NASHVILLE DREAMS

PAMELA M. KELLEY

PIPING PLOVER PRESS

Special thanks to Cindy Tahse, Irene Stovall, Jane and Taylor Barbagallo. Your support, encouragement and enthusiasm helped so much!

CHAPTER 1

Laura Scott patted her stomach and snuggled against her boyfriend, Cole Dawson. He tightened his arms around her and kissed her forehead gently as the warm, Charleston breeze danced over them. They were in their favorite spot, sprawled on the soft grass and leaning against the big old oak tree that overlooked a shallow pond where a family of swans floated along. They'd come here on their first official date, two years ago, after getting ice cream cones and strolling through the park. The old tree had beckoned to them and gave a bit of privacy as they watched people walking along the water's edge.

Laura sighed with happiness. On this sunny afternoon, a week after graduating from high school, she suddenly felt very adult and ready to take on the world, and relatively sure of her place in it. She glanced down at the modest diamond engagement ring she was wearing. Cole had given it to her a few days ago and she couldn't stop staring at it. Her mother had been thrilled, and relieved, considering.

Laura hadn't ever really worried, though, except for the initial day of panic when she learned the news and couldn't understand how it had happened, as they'd been so careful. Her doctor explained that the antibiotics she'd been taking for an ear infection had canceled out the birth control. She and Cole had already talked about getting married, though, and having children. She loved kids, and he said he wanted a houseful of them though neither one of them had expected to get started quite so early. It did change their plans a bit.

"I'll have to let Montana State know that I won't be attending after all. Hopefully, Clemson will still let me in." Laura was planning to be an elementary school teacher.

"Of course they will. They did accept you. And if it's too late for this year, you can do community college and then start up fresh in the fall."

"That could work. How do you think your father will take it? Do you want me to come with you?" Laura noticed a muscle clench in Cole's jaw and knew that he was dreading the conversation that he needed to have with his father.

"He's back tonight, and we're having dinner at the club. I thought that might be a good place to tell him. He can't go too crazy if we're out in public, especially there."

Cole's father could be intimidating, and although she'd offered to join Cole, to support him, Laura was actually glad that she wouldn't be there. As sure as Cole was about getting married, she knew that his father was going to give him a hard time about it.

Dalton Dawson was a big deal in Charleston. No one knew exactly how much he was worth, but it was rumored to be multiple billions. He was a real estate developer with holdings all over the country. He was smart, driven, and Laura suspected, a bit ruthless. She didn't particularly care for the man. He and Cole couldn't be more different. Where his father was hard and ambitious, Cole was sensitive, caring and creative. His dream was to be a country music artist.

Laura suspected that Cole took after his mother who had once been a singer, too. She'd never had the chance to meet her, as she'd died a year before she and Cole started dating, but he spoke of her often and had played some of her old recordings for Laura. She had a lovely voice. She had softened his father's edges, and they'd been madly in love. When she died, six months after being diagnosed with lung cancer, his father changed. He threw himself into work even more and recently found a new focus.

He was determined to be the next governor of South Carolina. Which was another reason he wasn't going to like their news. Dalton Dawson was a staunch Republican and conservative family values were a key part of his platform. His son knocking up a teenager who lived in a trailer park with her alcoholic mother wasn't going to go over well.

"He'll just have to deal with it. People have babies all the time, and at least we're getting married. I told him over a month ago that I was going to ask you to marry me so that won't be a surprise."

Laura chuckled. "He tried to talk you out of it, I imagine?"

"Well, yes. He said we're too young, for one thing." Cole looked like he was going to say something else, then thought better of it and Laura imagined that his father had shared a few more reasons as to why they're getting married wasn't a good idea. He didn't think she was good enough.

Cole reached into his pocket and drew out a Swiss army knife. He opened it and then smiled at Laura as he turned around and found the heart he'd carved into the old tree on their first date. It said *Laura and Cole* and the simple gesture had endeared him to her then. They'd seen each other almost every day since. Cole didn't care that she lived in a trailer park, and he liked her mother.

Cole was her best friend, and she couldn't imagine not having him in her life. She watched with curiosity as he carved something below their names. When he was done, he leaned back so she could see. It was a single word, in small letters so it could fit into the heart and it said, 'Forever'.

"There is nothing that my father can say that will change my mind. We are getting married as soon as possible. And then we're going to start the rest of our life together."

LAURA'S MOTHER was sitting on the patio smoking a cigarette when Cole dropped her off. He waved as he drove off, and Laura joined her mother and pulled up a chair. Technically where they lived was considered a mobile home, but there were no wheels. They were manufactured homes, modest but well-kept, and Laura had never minded living there. It was other people that seemed to mind, catty girls mostly, and as her mother had reminded her more than once if they had a problem with where she lived, that said more about their own issues.

As of a few years ago, her mother had paid off the mortgage and now owned her home free and clear. She was a tiny woman, just over five feet tall and about a hundred pounds. Laura smiled as she noticed that even after a long day of work, her mother's hair still looked good. That was one thing she envied about her. Unlike her own hair, which was long, fine and stick straight, her mother's was the same sandy blonde, but short and wavy and she didn't have to do a thing except run a comb through it.

She also had blue eyes, a cute nose, and an easy smile. She'd been beautiful when she was younger and in Laura's opinion, still was. She looked tired today, though. She worked as a waitress at a family restaurant and must have worked the lunch shift as she was still in her uniform and had a glass of Chablis by her side. Her mother enjoyed her wine and often had several glasses at the end of a long day.

"Has Cole told his father yet?" Her mother seemed worried. She knew as well as Laura did that Dalton Dawson was not going to be happy to hear the news.

"He's been out of town. They're talking tonight, at the club."

Her mother took a sip of wine and then a long drag on her cigarette.

"You don't have to get married, you know. You and the baby can stay here. There's room for all of us."

Laura reached out and squeezed her mother's arm. She knew that she really wouldn't mind having them stay. In fact, she'd probably love it. She had been about Laura's age when she found herself unexpectedly pregnant. Like Laura, she'd been madly in love and Richard, Laura's father, had felt the same. They'd married and everything had been wonderful, until a few years later when her father hurt his back on a construction site and became hooked on painkillers.

He died in his sleep one night after an accidental overdose which her mother blamed herself for and never really got over. Richard had been the love of her life, and though she occasionally went on a date, her heart wasn't in it. Laura worried that it might be hard for her when she moved out, and she was glad that Cole had agreed to stay in Charleston, so they would still be close to their families.

"Thank you. I think it will be okay, though. Cole is determined to get married, with or without his father's blessing."

CHAPTER 2

Cole met his father at the club. His father's office was right around the corner, and Cole was relieved to take his own car and not have to deal with the black mood his father was sure to be in. The Breville Country Club was the most exclusive club in Charleston. His father was a regular there and often held business meetings in the bar or over dinner.

Cole parked his old Volvo sedan in the parking lot and made his way into the club. It was an ostentatious place, and he'd never felt comfortable there. His father loved it. A marble entry-way opened into the lounge which had plush royal blue carpet, black leather seats, and polished dark wood. Cole found his father at the bar, chatting with several friends over a freshly poured martini. He smiled when he saw Cole.

"Right on time. What can I get you to drink?"

"I'll have a Coke.."

Mandy, the bartender, winked at Cole as she slid the soda toward him.

"Nice to see you, Cole. It's been a while," she said with a smile. Mandy had just graduated too and Cole had known her for years. He hadn't been to the club in a long time though. He used to golf more, but in recent months it hadn't been on his mind much.

"Thanks. It's been too long."

"You ready to sit down? Our table is ready whenever you are," his father said as his two friends paid their tab and left.

"Sure." As ready as he'd ever be. His father led them to a corner table by a window that faced out onto the course. Two menus were already there and the other two settings had been removed. They sat and his father took a long sip of his drink, looked like he was about to say something, then opened his menu instead.

A moment later, Edwin, the waiter that had been at the club for as long as Cole could remember, came by to tell them the specials and take their orders. They both always got the same thing—sirloin strip steaks, and a loaded baked potato. Once Edwin took their menus and left, his father turned to him.

"All right. Out with it. What's so important that we're having this conversation here?"

Cole took a deep breath. His father was still dressed for success in a rich tweed blazer and red silk tie, and he exuded power. He was tan, from spending the last week in the Bahamas and though he was in his early fifties, he had only a dusting of grey around his temples, which was mostly hidden by the gel he used on his thick, black hair.

"It's Laura. You know how I told you a month or so ago that we wanted to get married?"

His father scowled and reached for a hot roll as Edwin set a bread basket on the table with a tub of butter.

"I thought we decided that it was too soon for you to be thinking marriage? Better to wait until you are out of college. See if you're still even together then?" He slathered butter on his bread, took a bite and then added, "Maybe you'll find someone more...appropriate?"

Cole clenched his fist and fought the urge to smash something. He had to look away from the sneer on his father's face. When he spoke about Laura, it was as if he was thinking of something distasteful and it disgusted Cole.

"Dad, there is no one who is more appropriate for me than Laura."

"You say that now. You have to think of your future and where you are going, and choose a partner that will be an asset." He ripped off another piece of bread, and as he reached for the butter he added casually, "Bernie Thirwood told me just the other day that he'd be happy to have you join them when you finish law school."

Cole sighed. "I've never said I would go to law school. I don't think I want to be a lawyer."

His father set his butter knife down and slipped into his lecturing tone. "It's an excellent choice for you. It will give you options. Open doors for other things. If you major in tax law, that would be really helpful for the business. If you eventually decide to come on board."

"I don't see myself following in your footsteps, Dad. I'm sorry, but real estate development doesn't interest me."

"Well, what does, then? You're not still thinking foolish thoughts about Nashville and country music?"

"I am. That's my dream." Cole lifted his chin and met his father's eyes. "I'm good, too. People have said so."

His father laughed. "Who said that? Your girlfriend? And you wonder why I don't think she is a good choice for you." He shook his head. "You need to be practical, son. Play around with music all you want as a hobby. But you need a good education, a business degree at least, followed by law school."

"I'll think about it. Law school, that is. I am in for the business program." Cole figured it might not be a bad idea to make his father seem like he was going along with his recommendations. To calm him before they headed into stormy waters.

"Good. And I'm glad you decided on Clemson. Now, what's so important?"

Their meals arrived and Cole waited a moment, letting his father cut into his steak and take his first bite before proceeding to ruin his meal.

"Dad, we're going through with getting married, sometime over the next few weeks, and then we'll get a place together near Clemson."

"Why would you do that? I thought you said she was going out of state? Washington or Montana?"

He cut another bite of steak and Cole did the same,

and was just about to explain when his father set his fork down.

"She's pregnant?" His voice was cold, his eyes stormy as he glared at his son.

Cole nodded.

"This isn't good, for any of us."

Cole nodded again.

His father furrowed his brow and Cole knew he was scrambling for a solution, a way out.

"You know I'm considering a run for governor? People are telling me the time is right. I think it might be, too. But this isn't good. This is the kind of thing that won't reflect well on us. She lives in a trailer park, for God's sake."

"It's not like that. Not really. Where she lives is nice and neat."

"You can put lipstick on a pig, but everyone knows it's still a pig. It's a trailer park, no matter what else you want to call it."

"Fine, but still, there's nothing wrong with it."

"And she's pregnant and now you want to marry her. You should be starting your college years unencumbered, not with a baby on the way." He paused for a moment and then asked, "Will she consider an abortion?" He brightened as he said it and Cole cringed. His father was such a hypocrite.

"I didn't think you approved of that? That you were pro-life."

"Well, yes, I am. Of course, I am. But sometimes hard decisions must be made, for extenuating circumstances. As long as it's handled discreetly, no one needs to know."

"She doesn't want an abortion. Neither do I."

They finished their meals in silence. His father ordered another martini and checked emails on his phone while Cole gladly accepted another beer. When their plates were cleared, his father turned to him with an offer.

"If she agrees to get an abortion, I will pay for her to attend that school in Montana. I think that would be the best solution for everyone. If you still want to be together after you finish college, then so be it. But I think it would be a huge mistake for the two of you to have this baby. You'll run this by her, let her decide?"

Cole felt his meal threaten to come back up.

"She won't agree. I know her."

"That may be. But you'll ask her?"

"Fine. I'll ask her. But I wouldn't get your hopes up."

───────

"I THINK it's really sweet that Cole wants to come with you," Laura's mother said as they pulled up to the Dawson mansion. Laura had spoken to Cole briefly earlier that day. He'd called and confirmed that he still wanted to come for the doctor visit. Her doctor was going to do the first ultrasound, and they were both excited to see their baby.

Cole had sounded tense on the phone, though. She'd asked him how the dinner had gone the night before and all he'd said was that it had gone about as well as he'd expected and he'd fill her in later.

Laura jumped out to walk to the front door and get Cole while her mother waited in the car. Since it was the middle of the afternoon, she knew she wasn't likely to run into his father, but she was still nervous as she approached the front door. It was an intimidating house. It was huge, and they had live-in help. When Laura knocked on the door, it was opened by Sergio, their Brazilian butler. He broke into a wide smile when he saw Laura.

"Come on in, I'll tell Cole that you're here."

Laura stepped inside and waited in the foyer while Sergio went to get Cole. She glanced around at the sleek marble floors and soaring ceilings with elegant artwork on softly shaded walls. His house was gorgeous, but felt more like a museum than a home to her. She never said anything to Cole as it was all he knew, and it was beautiful. Just not what she would ever want. She heard footsteps and looked up to see him bounding down the stairs, a smile on his face.

"You're in a good mood," she said as he pulled her in for a quick kiss.

"I'm in a great mood. We're going to meet our baby for the first time. How cool is that?"

Laura relaxed a bit as they walked outside toward the car where her mother was smiling and waving at them. She'd trusted that Cole wouldn't let his father get to him, to change their plans, but still, the worry had been there. Dalton Dawson was a powerful and ruthless man, and she knew that he had never approved of her.

Laura got into the front seat and Cole settled into the back. They both buckled up as her mother pulled out of the driveway and onto the main road. The doctor's office was just a few miles away.

"Thanks for coming to get me," Cole said to her mother.

"Of course. I'm thrilled that you wanted to be there for Laura."

Traffic was light, and they were running a few minutes ahead of schedule. The last thing that any of them remembered was a large SUV that was going much too fast. It swerved into the opposite lane—and there was no time for her mother to react, to get out of the way. The SUV hit them head on, and in the span of just a few seconds, everything changed.

CHAPTER 3

"It's a shame about the mother," the doctor, Ted Holmes, said as he pressed his stethoscope on Cole's chest to listen to his breathing. Dalton Dawson knew him from the club. They played together in a league there.

"It didn't look good, from what I heard," Dalton agreed. When he'd gotten the initial call from the hospital two days ago, they had only said that Cole was one of three passengers in a fatal head-on collision and that he was being brought in to surgery.

"At least she died instantly. No suffering," Ted added as he moved on to check Cole's pulse. He seemed satisfied with what he was seeing.

"His vitals are good. He should pull through just fine, though he's going to be sore and not very mobile for a while. One of his ribs punctured a lung, and he had nasty breaks on both legs. He'll be here at least another week."

"How is Laura doing? And the baby?" Dalton asked casually.

"Well, she lost the baby, of course. The trauma was too much. Laura will be all right. She had very different injuries. A cracked tailbone and broken collarbone, deep lacerations along one side of her face and she hit her head pretty hard against the windshield. That's where the cuts came from. She had a severe concussion and there may have been some jarring to the brain, enough trauma to induce the worst case of memory loss that I've ever seen."

"Memory loss? Like amnesia?"

"Yes, exactly."

"Well, that's temporary, right? It should come back?"

"Hard to say. If she is in familiar surroundings, eventually it may come back. No guarantees, though. The brain is a tricky thing."

Dalton's thoughts began to spin, and possibilities to emerge.

"So, if she was in unfamiliar surroundings, there's a possibility that her amnesia could be permanent?"

The doctor thought about that for a moment. "Yes. I suppose so. In that case, she might never recover her memory at all."

"With her mother gone, there's no other family. I just found out a few days ago that she and Cole were engaged. As soon as she's well enough, I'd like to bring her home if that's all right. I'm heading out of town, but my sister can collect her."

"Of course," Ted agreed. "At least she has you, and Cole."

"Yes, well, please don't say anything to Cole about that. I want it to be a surprise when he gets home."

The doctor smiled. "That should cheer him up, I would imagine."

Dalton nodded, and then casually asked, "Has anything been said to Laura about her mother or the baby?"

The doctor paused. "No, not yet. We were waiting to see if she might ask first. To see if her memory was coming back."

"Can you leave that to us, too? We can break it to her at a later time. When she's stronger."

"That sounds like a wonderful plan to me. She's lucky to have you both."

Laura woke and was dismayed to find that she was still in the hospital. She stretched and glanced out the window. The sun was shining and tall trees just outside her window swayed in the breeze. It was a beautiful, serene day, but Laura felt the same panic rising that she'd felt for each of the last two days when she'd woken and had no idea where she was or why she was there. No one had given her much information.

All she knew was that she knew that she'd been in an accident, a bad one, and she was still feeling foggy. She didn't remember any of the details. Not who she'd been with, or where they were going. It was puzzling, and scary. And the harder she tried to remember, the more confused and alone she felt. She turned at the sound of footsteps entering the room.

"There you are. I came as quickly as I could. I was so worried."

Laura looked at the pleasant-faced, fifty-something woman and felt as though she should know who she was, but she was drawing a complete blank.

"You don't remember me, do you?" the woman asked softly.

Laura stared at her miserably. She was trying so hard to remember but failing utterly.

The woman walked over and lightly kissed her cheek, then took hold of one of her hands.

"I'm your Aunt Helen, honey. Your mom's sister." She paused for a moment and then continued. "You've lived with me for almost eighteen years, in Bozeman, Montana."

"Montana?" Laura asked. It sounded so foreign to her. And confusing. "What am I doing here, then? When I watch the news, it says Charleston, South Carolina."

The woman smiled. "That's right, honey. We were just passing through on our way back from a trip to Florida. There was a bad accident. Unfortunately, you got the worst of it. I booked us tickets to fly home from here today."

Laura's head started to hurt. It was a lot to process.

"Why aren't we driving?"

"The doctor thought it might be too hard on your tail-bone, all that riding in the car. You sprained it pretty badly. I'm having the car shipped home."

"We're leaving today?" Laura asked, feeling panicky

again. This woman who said she was her Aunt Helen didn't look remotely familiar to her. But then she smiled again, and Laura relaxed. There was something faintly familiar about that smile. She felt the tension ease out of her body.

"I'm going to go get a coffee and give you time to change. The doctor should be in shortly with your discharge papers." Aunt Helen wandered off, and Laura eased out of bed and checked the time. The clock on the wall read almost ten a.m. She never slept that late. At least she didn't think that she did. She found a clear plastic bag on a side counter that held a pair of shorts and a pink t-shirt. Laura was dismayed to see that the t-shirt had a bloody gash at the neckline. The doctor had told her that she'd fractured her collarbone, so she supposed that made sense. She turned suddenly at the sound of footsteps coming in the room again.

"I'm sorry, honey, I meant to give this to you a few minutes ago. I brought along a fresh pair of sweatpants and a sweatshirt for you." She handed Laura the clean clothes.

"Thank you. This is perfect."

Aunt Helen smiled. "Great. I'll be right back, then. Do you want anything? Coffee, tea?"

Laura thought for a minute. "I'd love an iced coffee, actually. Extra cream and sugar, please."

That was strange. She didn't remember liking iced coffee, but somehow knew how she took it. She hoped that was a good sign and that the rest of her memory would soon come back.

Laura heard voices outside the door, and then her aunt and Dr. Holmes walked in together.

She took a sip of the iced coffee that her aunt handed her while the doctor shuffled a stack of papers and then handed several of them to her.

"These are your discharge instructions. Take it easy for the next few weeks. Don't put any unusual pressure on your tailbone. Don't try too hard to remember. Let your memories come back when they are ready. Sound good?"

Laura nodded.

"I bet you're ready to get going," the doctor said with a smile. He nodded to Aunt Helen and then was on his way.

"Are you ready, honey? Our flight is in three hours, so we need to get a move on."

COLE WAS SLEEPING when Dalton arrived later that day. His sister Helen had called from the airport just before she and Laura caught their flight. She said that things had gone smoothly and Laura accepted her story. She gave him hell for it, too, and he supposed he couldn't blame her. But she owed him.

He looked down at his son who looked so peaceful, his body broken and sore. He felt a twinge of guilt. He knew his bones would heal quickly, but his heart would take a bit longer. It was a blessing that they'd lost the baby. They were too young. He was convinced that it was just puppy love and that Cole was destined for greater things. He shouldn't be tied down with a wife at his age. He needed to go to college, to enjoy life and then to make a suitable, smart match.

Cole woke up, rubbed his eyes and then sat up when he saw his father leaning against the windowsill.

"When did you get here?" he asked sleepily.

"Just a few minutes ago. How're you feeling?"

Cole stretched and then grimaced. "Stiff and a little sore. They said it should ease up in a few more days."

"I talked to the doctor on the way in. He thinks you should be able to go home tomorrow."

Cole smiled. "That's great. I'm ready." His faced clouded, and Dalton knew what was coming next.

"How's Laura? I don't understand why she hasn't been in to see me?" He sounded hurt and worried. Dalton couldn't put it off any longer.

"She's gone, son. They released her today, and she left with her aunt."

"What aunt? Go where?"

"Well, she lost the baby, you know..." Dalton began, and Cole cut him off impatiently.

"Yes, I know that. It was the first thing I asked once I found out Laura was okay."

"Right. Well, here's the thing. You might be a little mad at me, and I wouldn't say I blamed you, but just know I did this for you, and for your future."

"What are you talking about?" Cole glared at his father. "What did you do?"

Dalton sighed. "I've told you before that she's not right

for you. I offered her money. Offered to pay for her college plus enough extra that she won't have to worry about money anytime soon. She's never had that before."

"Laura doesn't care about money."

"Everyone cares about money. Especially people who have never had it before. I offered her a life-changing amount."

"If she goes away and has nothing to do with me?"

"Well, yes. That's what the money is for. It was a test, son. I almost didn't think she was going to say yes. But, as it turns out the old saying is right. Everyone has a price."

"I don't believe it. Where is she? I want to hear it from her."

"I don't know where she went. That was part of the deal, for her to disappear and get out of your life completely."

"That's ridiculous. Where's my cell phone? I can call her at least."

"You can try, but she may have blocked you or changed her number. That was a requirement before we gave her the check. We had to be sure."

"Give me my phone."

Dalton handed Cole his phone, watching as he searched for Laura's number and then dialed it. Hope turned to horror as the recorded message came on saying the number had been disconnected.

"I can't believe you did this to me. Do you hate me that much?" The raw hurt on his son's face made Dalton take a step back and for just a moment, he second-guessed his actions. But what was done was done and in his heart of hearts, he believed it was for the best.

"I did this because I love you."

CHAPTER 4

Laura was exhausted by the time their plane touched down in Bozeman. She'd had a window seat and gazed at the mountains in awe as they descended. They were beautiful, breath-taking even, and it was like she was seeing them for the first time. It was the same when they were in a cab riding to her aunt's house. Not a single street or landmark looked familiar, and she strained her memory trying to remember. By the time they reached her aunt's house, she had a full-blown headache.

"You look tired, honey. Why don't you go lay down when we get inside? Take a nap before dinner. The doctor said you might be achy and weak for a few days from the anesthesia. I've always felt like I have the flu after any kind of surgery. Some people are more sensitive to it than others."

"I am pretty tired. Maybe I will lay down for a bit."

The cab pulled into the driveway, and her aunt paid the driver and then they went inside. A feeling of panic came over Laura when nothing in the house looked familiar. It truly felt like she was stepping inside for the first time.

It was a lovely house. The walls were painted in soft, soothing shades of pale blues and greens. The kitchen was to the right, and was bright and clean with white cabinets and practical Formica countertops. The floors were hardwood, topped with cheery throw rugs in pastel shades. Laura looked down the hallway, guessing that one of the rooms was her bedroom as the house was a modest, single floor ranch. Her aunt smiled at her, but Laura couldn't miss the look of concern. She seemed uncomfortable, a bit nervous even and Laura guessed it must be because of her faulty memory.

"Your room is the one at the end. Why don't you go relax and I'll have some chicken soup ready for us later for supper?" Chicken soup and a nap sounded good to Laura. She made her way down the hall and into the room at the end. It was a nice room, with a soft peach comforter on a queen-sized bed, and a white fleece blanket neatly folded across the foot of it. There were a few paintings on the wall. It reminded Laura of a guest room as it didn't seem to have much life to it.

She opened a closet and saw an assortment of clothes, most of which looked relatively new, which seemed odd. She checked the drawers of the bureau and noticed the same thing—underwear neatly folded and looking as though it had never been worn. She heard footsteps coming down the hall and looked up to see her aunt standing in the doorway.

"I realized that probably looks strange to you. We just moved in here two weeks ago and there was a mix-up the day we moved. Several trash bags full of your clothes were accidentally thrown out. We didn't realize it until it was too late. But the good news is you have all new clothes, and we can go out tomorrow and finish shopping. We only had time to get the basics before it was time to leave for our trip."

"Oh, all right. That makes sense." Laura yawned. She was suddenly so very tired.

"Go ahead and climb into bed...I'll check on you later." Her aunt shut the door behind her and Laura slowly made her way to the bed, slipped off her shoes, and then stretched out on the soft comforter and pulled the fleece blanket over her. She closed her eyes and tried to will away the panicky feeling that kept rising. The doctor had said that amnesia like hers was common after head injuries and that being around people and places that were familiar should help her get it back sooner rather than later. She tried not to dwell on the fact that so far, nothing here felt familiar. She hoped in time that it would.

Laura woke several hours later and noticed that it was starting to get dark outside. She stretched and her stomach grumbled as she remembered her aunt mentioning something earlier about chicken soup. She was just swinging her legs out of bed when there was a soft knock on her door and her aunt poked her head inside.

"Oh good, you're up. I'm just putting the soup out if you'd like to join me."

Laura followed her out to the kitchen, and they sat at a round table in a nook area that overlooked a grassy backyard.

"I almost forgot the bread." Her aunt jumped up and pulled a foil-wrapped loaf of bread from the oven, took the foil off, and set it on a plate and brought it over to the table where there was already a tub of butter. The bread was crunchy on the outside, and soft and warm inside. Laura cut herself a thick slice and added a generous amount of butter. As they ate, her aunt mentioned that she wanted to visit her son, Harold, in a few days.

"He's a little older than you, almost twenty-three, but mentally he's two. He needs around the clock care and he's in a special home, with two others like him and they have a team of caregivers. He's been there for a few months now and it seems to be working out well. I wanted to make sure before I made the commitment to move closer.

He's been at other places that haven't worked out as well. He's a wonderful child. But he's challenging and the older he gets, the more care he requires and more health issues crop up. He's already outlived the typical life expectancy for people with his condition."

"What is his condition?" Laura asked.

"Several genetic disorders, including Downs Syndrome and autism."

Laura thought about that for a moment. She tried hard to remember Harold but her mind was completely blank.

"Where did we live before this?"

"Several hours north. Just outside Billings. You're all set to go to Montana State in the fall."

"I am?" That sounded vaguely familiar to Laura, which cheered her up a bit. She was confident that her memory would soon be back.

"Tomorrow we can ride around a bit and explore the area. It's still new to me as well. There's a strip mall a few miles down the road. A few of the stores there had help wanted signs up, and you mentioned applying when we got back from our vacation."

"Oh? That's a great idea." With several months of summer stretching out before her, Laura welcomed a part-time job to keep busy.

"What did I decide to major in?"

Her aunt looked stumped for a moment, trying to remember.

"Liberal Arts, I think. No, that's not right. Education, maybe? You can change it, though. See how you feel when you get there and start taking classes."

Laura yawned. Even though she'd had a nap, she still felt exhausted. It had been a long day and a lot to process.

"I think I might go to bed early," she said.

Her aunt smiled. "That's a good idea. We'll get an early start in the morning."

LAURA GOT a good night's sleep, and she and her aunt spent the next day exploring Bozeman, shopping for more clothes, enjoying lunch at a local cafe and filling out applications at the three businesses that were hiring at the strip mall her aunt had mentioned. There was a music shop that sold all kinds of instruments as well as CDs and also gave guitar lessons, a hair salon that was looking for a receptionist, and a bakery that needed counter help. Laura spoke briefly to the managers at each place and all said they would be in touch soon, They asked for her availability, which she said was immediate.

Once they were in the car and on their way home, her aunt asked her if she had a preference between the three places.

Laura laughed. "Not really. If any of them call and offer me a job, the answer is yes."

THE NEXT DAY, they went to visit Harold. Laura noticed that her aunt seemed anxious as they pulled into the parking lot and made their way to the townhouse where Harold lived. She relaxed and broke into a big smile when a slightly chubby, dark-haired young man ran over to her as soon as they walked in.

"Mama! Mama!" He flung himself at her and wrapped his arms around her waist. She hugged him back tightly and Laura noticed that her eyes were damp.

"Hi, Sweetie. Have you been a good boy? We missed you."

"Painting," Harold said in response, and pulled his mother over to the table where he'd been sitting with two others, all using crayons to color.

"Harold loves to color, though he calls it painting." A young woman in her mid-twenties walked over to them and her aunt introduced her. "Laura this is Carol, Harold's main caregiver. Carol, this is Harold's cousin, Laura. I wanted to wait until he was settled in here before bringing her by to visit."

Carol nodded. "It's nice to meet you." She turned back to her aunt. "It's been a pretty good week. Some ups and downs, but mostly good."

Her aunt looked concerned. "Is he having stomach issues again?"

"Yes, we've been adjusting his medicine to see if that helps. The doctor was in a few days ago and said this is normal, unfortunately, and there's not a lot to be done, except to manage the symptoms as best we can."

Her aunt sighed. "He looks good. Laura, let's go over and say hello."

"I'll be in the other room if you need me," Carol said. She wandered off, and they went over to visit with Harold. He was coloring happily and looked up when they drew closer.

"Harold, you remember your cousin, Laura?"

He just smiled at her.

"Hi, Harold. You're doing a good job there," Laura said.

He beamed. "Painting!" and then focused back on his crayons and paper.

They stayed for another hour or so and then said their goodbyes to Harold, who looked up for a moment. When when he realized they were leaving, he ran to his mother and hugged her tightly and started to seem agitated.

"Mama! Mama!" he screamed and then the tears came. Carol came rushing out at the sound, drew Harold away and gave him a big hug. He rocked back and forth and kept screaming, "Mama! Mama!" over and over again.

"Go ahead. I've got him. He'll settle down as soon as he can't see you. Don't worry." Carol spoke softly and Laura held the front door open for her aunt, who also had tears streaming down her cheeks as they walked out.

"Is it always like that?" Laura asked, once they were in the car and her aunt had calmed down and found a tissue to dry her eyes.

"Yes. It seems like he hardly knows we're there, but then when I try to leave, he gets upset. It breaks my heart every time."

"How long has he been living away from home?" Laura asked, curious about why Harold wasn't living at home.

"It's been three years now. It was the hardest decision I've ever had to make. Ultimately, it's for the best, but it's still painful. He needs more attention and care than I could give him, without quitting my job to stay home full-time and even then, it would be too much for one person. He's gotten worse as he's gotten older and requires constant monitoring. I did it for as long as I could. Longer than was recommended, but it was so hard to let him go." She pressed her tissue to her eyes again and then shifted into reverse and backed out of her parking spot.

"He didn't seem to remember me," Laura said.

Her aunt was quiet for a moment and then said, "It's been a few months since he's seen you. We wanted to get him settled first. He doesn't recognize most people unless he's with them all the time."

"How often do you see him?"

"I go every weekend, both days usually."

Laura nodded. "I'll go with you this weekend. Maybe he'll recognize me then."

When they got home, there were two messages on the machine. The first was from the music shop. The store manager, Peter, asked her to call as soon as she got the message. The second was from the bakery, also asking her to call and ask for Julie, the owner.

"Which one are you going to take?" Her aunt asked.

"I'll call them both, but if the music shop is offering a job, I'll take it since they called first."

Peter answered on the first ring and got right to the point. "I'd love to hire you if you're interested. It'll be three or four shifts a week, late afternoon to close which is at seven. Weekends we close at six."

"That sounds great."

"You said you were available immediately. Is tomorrow too soon? I could have you shadow me for a shift."

"Tomorrow's fine."

"See you at three, then." Laura hung up the phone and went to make her second call.

"Congratulations!" her aunt said.

"Thank you. Would it be crazy, do you think, if I accepted both jobs? The bakery will mostly be breakfast and lunch I think."

"As long as you don't think it will be too much, I don't see why not. See what they say."

Laura spoke with Julie, who also offered her a position working the counter and said the hours were usually mornings and sometimes included lunch, but they closed at two, so she'd easily be able to walk a few doors down to be to the music shop by three. Julie also said she could use her several days a week, so the two jobs combined would be like one full-time position. Laura hung up the phone and smiled. She now had something to do with her days.

CHAPTER 5

Cole was miserable. Everywhere he went, people asked about Laura and all he could tell them was that they'd broken up and she'd moved out of state with a distant relative since she had no other family in the area. But he was supposed to be her family. Cole had no idea who this distant relative was or where she might have gone. As far as he knew, her mother was the only family that she had. He didn't have much of a family at the moment, either, as he wasn't speaking to his father.

He had plenty of friends, of course, and kept busy with them. He worked at the club as a caddy and played a lot of golf, taking care to avoid the times when he knew his father would be there. He was looking forward to the fall and college. It was bittersweet, though, as he'd assumed that both he and Laura would be attending together and that they'd be newlyweds by then with a baby on the way. He'd been a little freaked out at first about the idea of having children so young. But the idea had grown on him, and he'd thought that he and Laura could handle anything because their love was strong. He still couldn't understand how he could have been so wrong about that.

Part of him blamed his father, of course, for paying her to go away. But the other part of him argued that if she took the money, then she wasn't the one for him. Their love wasn't as strong as he'd thought it was. One thing he knew for sure was that he wasn't going to be in a hurry to get married to anyone anytime soon. He was still feeling numb and raw. He didn't even really feel like dating at all, but his friends kept encouraging him to get back out there. To get back on the horse and get over it. Easier said than done. But he sensed that it might be a good idea to just have fun, make it clear he wasn't looking to be serious and just casually date.

So he did. He went out with a few different girls but and rarely saw anyone more than once or twice. They were all nice girls, but they were interchangeable to him, just pleasant company to pass the time and try to get his mind off the one woman he wanted but could never have again.

HER AUNT SAID that there was car in the garage that Laura could use. Her husband had loved old convertibles and she hadn't been able to bring herself to sell it. She drove it every now and then to keep it going. Laura would have to take a driving test to get her license first though. That surprised her a little as she felt like she already knew how to drive. Her aunt said she'd been teaching her before they went on vacation. But, at least the music shop was close enough that she could walk there until then.

When Laura arrived at the shop, Peter was ringing up a customer at the register. As soon as he finished, he showed Laura around and taught her to use the register and how to look up artists in the store database online.

"People often come in and know what they're looking for but don't remember the name of the song or of the band. We can usually figure it out with what they do remember and point them in the right direction."

He showed her the various instruments. They had the biggest selection of guitars, and he explained how they differed from each other.

"We also give lessons, mostly on guitar, but some piano, too. Did I mention that one perk of the job is free lessons?" He grinned. "It helps if you're familiar with the different guitars so you can steer customers in the right direction and answer some of their questions. It also gives us something to do during slow times. Which one do you want to try?"

"Right now? I can try any of them?"

"Pick your favorite."

Laura walked around the shop looking closely at the different guitars until finally selecting one of the smaller ones.

"An excellent choice. That's one of the entry-level guitars, one that people often start out with. It's less expensive and is great to learn the basics on. Grab a pick from that bowl by the counter and come sit next to me."

Laura did as he asked, selecting a hot pink pick and

then brought the guitar over to where Peter was already seated with his own guitar. She sat next to him and for the next twenty minutes until a customer walked in, Peter showed her the basics, how to hold her hands and use the pick and how to play several chords.

"Keep practicing. You're doing great. Billy is here for a lesson, so we're heading out back. Think you can hold down the fort for the next half hour?"

"Sure."

"Good. If you need help, just holler, and I'll come out."

Peter and Billy went off to the back for their lesson and Laura played around with the guitar until another customer came in. She was surprised by how much she liked the feel of the instrument and the strings against her fingers. She also liked the way the chords sounded as she played one after another. She found an instruction book on a shelf nearby and taught herself several more chords. She knew that she'd never played guitar before, but something about it felt so familiar, as if she somehow instinctively knew how to make music. For the first time since she'd come to Montana, she started to feel a spark of excitement, a thrill of discovery.

She set the guitar down and jumped up when a customer came through the door.

"Do you have the newest Pearl Jam CD? I'm drawing a blank on the name." The customer, a man in his early thirties, asked.

"Let me check." Laura looked in the database and saw that they had two copies in stock.

"We have it. I'll show you where it is." She led him to

the aisle and found the two CDs exactly where they should be.

"Great, thanks!"

As Laura was ringing up the sale, Peter and Billy walked towards her. She handed the man his change and CD in a small paper bag and said, "Thank you,"

Billy waved goodbye, and Peter turned to her.

"Everything go all right? Looked like you were doing fine with the register."

"He bought the new Pearl Jam CD. I hope you don't mind, but I looked through that instruction book and taught myself a few more chords."

"You did? Let's hear."

Laura picked up the guitar and nervously played the chords she'd taught herself. When she finished, she looked to Peter for feedback and was relieved to see that he was smiling.

"You're a natural. Let me show you a few more things."

The rest of the shift flew, and Peter walked her out when they closed the shop at seven.

"You did a great job today. I have you off tomorrow but will see you at three the next day. Sound good?"

Laura smiled. "Yes, thank you. See you then."

She climbed onto her bike, and ten minutes later pulled into her aunt's driveway and led the bike into the garage. As she was leaning it against the garage wall, she noticed something in a far corner and walked over to investigate. There was a guitar there, covered with dust and sticking out of a box. In the box were stacks of sheet music and what looked like a very old instruction manual. She wondered whose guitar it had been. Did her aunt play? Surely it wasn't Harold's? She picked it up and liked the feel of the wood. It was about the same size as the one she'd been playing in the shop. She rubbed away some of the dust and saw that the guitar itself seemed to be in good condition. She strummed it and grabbed a pick from the bottom of the box. Dusty or not, the guitar sounded just fine as she tried out a few of the chords she'd just learned. She suddenly felt ridiculously happy as she set the guitar back in the box and then went inside to ask her aunt about it.

"THAT WAS your uncle Jim's. My husband." Her eyes grew cloudy, and Laura sensed the sadness surrounding her like a cloak. "He died of colon cancer five years ago. Just three months after being diagnosed."

"I'm so sorry." They were sitting at the kitchen table, and Laura glanced at the photo on the wall.

"That's him." Her aunt, and a pleasant-faced, brown-haired man that didn't look at all familiar to Laura, were sitting by a lake. It was a lovely picture, and it frustrated Laura. Why couldn't she remember these people? Her aunt reached out and patted her hand.

"It's strange but normal not to remember. The doctor said that you might not get all of your memories back. You'll just have to create new ones."

Laura smiled. "I know. I keep reminding myself of that."

"Why don't you bring it in? It must be awfully dusty. I

don't play, and I almost tossed it out when we moved, but I couldn't bring myself to do it. He loved that guitar. He was pretty good, too. There was some music and books with it too, I think?"

"Yes, everything was in a box out there. You don't mind if I bring it in? I just had my first lesson at work today, and it would be fun to play with it."

"No, I don't mind at all. It would be wonderful to see someone getting some joy out of it."

———

Laura woke early the next morning to get to the bakery by six a.m. Julie, the owner, was there when she arrived and unlocked the front door to let her in. Julie was in her late thirties, with short, spiky black hair and bright green eyes. She had told Laura when she met with her initially that she and her husband bought the bakery five years ago and he did most of the baking while she managed the front of the restaurant.

"Do many people come in this early?" Laura asked as she followed Julie out back and then tied on the pink apron that she handed her. It had big pockets in front and a strap that went around her neck.

"Quite a few, actually. Mostly people who start their jobs early and stop in for a coffee or muffin first. Or some retired folks that are up early and like to meet up with their friends and socialize. You'll get to know most of them," Julie said as she showed her how to work the coffee and espresso machines.

"You'll also answer the phone, which is next to the register, and take any to-go orders. They tend to come in spurts, usually when we are the busiest."

When they went back out front, a pretty girl with a blonde ponytail came flying through the door.

"I'm so sorry that I'm late." The words came out in a rush. Julie smiled and introduced them

"Laura, this is Tina. She's a recent high school grad, too."

"Nice to meet you," Tina said as she ran by them to put her stuff out back.

"You'll like Tina. She has a hard time getting here on time, but she's a great waitress, and the customers love her. When the counter isn't busy, you can help her and I'll be able to use you as a waitress, too, if you're interested?"

"I'd love that. I'll do anything."

Julie smiled. "I like that attitude. You'll make more money waitressing, but you'll earn it, too."

For the first two hours, it wasn't very busy, and Laura was glad for it as it gave her a chance to get familiar with the bakery before the breakfast rush came in. It also let her chat a bit with Tina, and she discovered that she was also going to Montana State in the fall.

"What are you majoring in?" Tina asked during a rare quiet moment when no one needed them.

"Education, I think. For now, anyway."

Tina raised her eyebrow. "Having second thoughts about that major?"

"Sort of," Laura admitted. "I signed up for it, but I may switch to Liberal Arts as I have no idea what I want to do."

"You could join me in Business. That's a broad major, and my father said it will give me more options." She grinned. "I have no idea what I want to do when I get out, either. Something fun, maybe, like marketing."

The rest of the day flew once the breakfast rush started, and before Laura knew it, it was two o'clock.

"See you tomorrow," Tina called out as she left, and Laura climbed onto her bike and rode home.

The house was empty when she arrived. Her aunt was back to work. She worked for an attorney's office as a legal secretary and had worked for the company for over twenty years. She said that she liked the work, and the people were nice.

Laura made herself a cup of lemon tea and then took it to her bedroom. Her first urge was to lay down on the bed and give in to the wave of sadness that seemed to wash over her every day at some point. It usually happened when she slowed down, and no one else was around. It was tempting to curl up in a ball and give in to it, but she didn't understand where it was coming from and she wanted it to just stop. As long as she kept busy, the bewildering emptiness seemed to stay away. She sensed that it had something to do with the accident.

Every now and then, out of the corner of her eye, she noticed her aunt watching her carefully with a look of concern. She never said anything, though, and Laura never brought up the strange episodes of sadness that came over her. She didn't want to upset her aunt and doubted there was anything she could do about them.

She was glad that she'd decided to take both jobs. The

people at both places seemed nice enough, and the work was interesting. Most importantly, it gave her something to do, to keep her too busy to feel sad. She walked over to the guitar leaning against the wall by her bed. She picked it up and played the chords she'd learned, both the ones that Peter taught her and the ones she'd learned herself. She smiled and she felt the sadness ebb as the joy of the music took hold. The hours fell away as she practiced what she'd learned the day before and played around teaching herself two more chords using the book she'd found in the garage.

For the first time since the accident, she slept peacefully and woke feeling energized. Over the next few weeks, she fell into a routine of going from one job to the next, visiting Harold with her aunt on the weekends. She and Tina became fast friends and often went out with a crowd of girls and boys that Tina went to school with. Laura quickly became friends with all of them and the periods of sadness came less frequently. She enjoyed the fast pace of the bakery and the camaraderie of working with Tina and the other waitresses, but she loved her time at the music shop. The pace there was slower, and she discovered a real passion and talent for music.

Peter worked with her whenever it was slow and was thrilled with how quickly she seemed to be picking things up.

"Guitar isn't an easy instrument to learn. And I've noticed that you seem to have a natural ear for the melodies. Do you find yourself able to reproduce songs that you hear?"

Laura smiled. "Yes, I've just started to play with doing

that. Now that I'm comfortable with the chords, I'm starting to recognize them when I hear songs played and I've been trying to play what I remember."

"Not many people can do that. You really seem to have a gift for this." He grinned.

"You should try to write a song now."

"What? I wouldn't know where to begin," Laura said with a chuckle.

"Start paying attention to the rhythm of some of the songs you like. There are patterns to all of them, chorus lines that are repeated. Try it both ways. Think of some lines, then find music to wrap around them. Or find a melody you like and then find the right words for it. There's no right or wrong way."

"Do you write songs?" Laura asked. She was intrigued by the idea.

"I do. Tell you what. You go home tonight and write something. Anything. Don't worry about it being good or even making sense. Just play with the words and find a melody you like. Bring it in tomorrow and we'll play for each other. Deal?"

"I don't know," Laura hesitated.

"Oh come on. It's something to do. Aren't you getting tired of practicing the same chords over and over?"

Laura chuckled. "All right. I'll give it a try. It might be really bad, though."

"No worries. You have to start somewhere."

CHAPTER 6

"How is she?" Dalton asked as soon as his sister answered the phone. He'd waited a month to call, figuring there would be an adjustment period and if it was going to blow up in his face, he knew he would have heard from Helen by now.

"She's a lovely girl. She's working two jobs, visits Harold with me on the weekends and is looking forward to starting school in the fall. She's actually a delight to have around." They were both silent for a moment, and then she added, "You could do much worse, you know, for Cole. She would have made him a wonderful wife. Even at their young age."

Dalton cleared his throat. He didn't appreciate being scolded by his older sister.

"Yes, well, you said it. They were too young. This is the best thing for both of them."

"You really believe that? You couldn't trust the two of them to make up their own minds?"

"No. Neither one of them was thinking straight. They were getting married because of the baby. With the baby gone, they would have still gotten married out of guilt or something,"

"Love?" Helen suggested.

Dalton sighed. "They think it's love, I know. But they'd be throwing their whole lives away. Now they can start fresh."

"You don't think she's good enough. Because of where she came from."

"As you said, she is a lovely girl, but if they'd married, people would have talked. They probably would have gotten pregnant again and it just wouldn't reflect well on the family."

"On you, you mean and your campaign for governor?"

"He'll be glad for this in the long run. Both of them will. Now they can both start college fresh and enjoy all that it has to offer. Cole would never have gone to law school with a baby in tow."

"He's going to law school?" His sister sounded surprised.

"Well, he hasn't agreed to it yet, but it would be an excellent career choice for him."

"Do you even know what he really wants to do?"

"You mean the country music nonsense? He'll get over that."

"He wants a career in music? That's interesting." Helen sounded surprised and contemplative.

"Does he play the guitar?" she asked.

"Funny you should ask. I'd refused to get him one

before. I didn't want to encourage this. But after the accident, he's been so down in the dumps that I surprised him with one a few weeks ago. Thought it would cheer him up, but now I see him even less. He's always in his room playing the damn thing."

"I think it's good that you got him one. Maybe he'll get it out of his system, or maybe he'll be good at it? You never know..."

Dalton shuddered at the thought. "Not if I have anything to say about it. I told him I don't mind if he plays as a hobby, but he needs to focus on a real career. He'd make a great lawyer."

"I'm sure he'll be great at whatever he chooses to do."

Dalton decided to change the subject.

"So, the girl's good? No sudden flashes of memory? I don't need her remembering now..."

His sister sighed. "I don't think you need to worry about that. She hasn't mentioned a thing. I think the doctor was right. She doesn't know anyone here. She really is starting over."

"Well, she's a lucky girl. She won't have any student loans to worry about. That wouldn't be the case if her mother were still around."

"I'm sure she'd much rather have her mother...if she remembered her."

The scolding tone was back. He'd had enough of it for one day.

"All right, then. It's been good talking to you."

"Goodbye, Dalton."

He hung up the phone and stared out the window,

suppressing the twinge of guilt that briefly visited when he thought of Laura or his sister. He'd basically forced her to do this. Harold's care was expensive, and Helen hadn't wanted to be a part of this at all until he'd promised to take over all of Harold's expenses. He figured it was short money in the long run as Harold was already past his life expectancy. He didn't say it to his sister, but he doubted that he'd be around in a few more years.

He tapped his finger on his desk. His mammoth desk was made of the finest wood, polished to a brilliant sheen. With Cole on his way to college, and Laura thousands of miles away, there was nothing to get in the way of his plans. And Dalton had big plans. He'd been a success in business, but he needed a new challenge, and the allure of politics had been beckoning for some time. He'd flirted with the idea of running for a senate seat, but some of his more connected colleagues had advised him that the governor's role might be a better fit and a more effective launchpad should he decide to pursue any national ambitions, even ultimately run for president. He'd laughed off the idea modestly and said that he wanted to focus on one thing at a time. But who was he kidding? That would be the ultimate goal and one that wouldn't have been possible if his son had married someone who grew up in a trailer park.

LAURA FOUND a few blank sheets of paper from a desk in the kitchen and brought them to her room. She wasn't sure where to start, with the music or the words. Or what to write about. She settled on the edge of her bed, picked up the guitar and a pick and with her eyes closed started strumming. She played various chords, experimenting with how different sounds went together and stopping now and then to jot down what she'd just played, so she'd remember later. After a bit, she looked at the notes on the paper, and suddenly, she wasn't sure where they came from, but words appeared. She wrote them down and then sang them softly as she played her favorite bits of music with them. She made some edits and then tried again, and then again. Until she heard her aunt's car pull in the driveway. She wasn't finished yet, but she had enough down that she could pick it up again after dinner and fine tune. She knew it was rough, but it was the most fun she'd had in ages, and she was excited and nervous to share it with Peter.

The following afternoon, she finished up her shift at the bakery, chatted with Tina for a bit, then took off her apron, pulled her stack of scribbled papers out of the tote bag she brought with her, and walked over to the music shop. Peter was ringing up a customer when she arrived and after he gave him his change, he turned to Laura.

"Billy had to cancel his lesson today, so we have an hour before the next one is scheduled." His eyes lit up as he grabbed his favorite guitar.

"You ready to play a little?"

Laura nodded, and he handed her the guitar she usually practiced on.

"How did you do? Did you come up with anything?" he asked.

"I did. It's rough, but I had a good time with it. It was really fun."

Peter smiled as he started to lightly strum his guitar.

"That's awesome. Tell you what. I'll go first and you'll see how outrageously bad my song is, and yours will seem brilliant by comparison."

Laura laughed and sat back to listen as he played a silly tune about his dog, Shep.

"That was good!" she said when he finished.

"It's not going to win any awards, but I had fun with it. That's all that matters." He leaned back and set his guitar down. "All right. Your turn."

Laura swallowed nervously as she unfolded her sheets of paper and laid them on the counter to her side. She didn't really need them. She had the music and the lyrics memorized now, she'd played it so many times. But it was reassuring to have there, anyway. She played a few chords and then started to lightly sing, her voice growing stronger as she went along. The song was a haunting, pretty tune about love and loss, and she really didn't know where it came from. But it felt right, and she liked the way it had turned out. When she finished, she glanced up to see Peter looking at her intently. And then he clapped.

"That was really something. You wrote that yourself?" His voice held a mixture of awe and confusion.

"I don't really know what it's about, it's just some things that came to mind. I spent most of the afternoon and evening working on it, playing with the melody. I got that part first and then the words came, sort of in a rush. And then I went back and forth, tweaking the words and the notes here and there until it felt right."

Peter smiled and shook his head. "Well, however you did it, it worked. See if you can do it again."

Laura glowed. She was thrilled the Peter had liked her song. She had felt that it might not be bad but really wasn't sure. It was great to get that kind of feedback. Those hours she'd spent in the zone, writing that song, was like nothing she'd ever experienced before. It was pure bliss, and she couldn't wait to do it again.

PLAYING the guitar was harder than Cole had imagined it would be. It frustrated him because he'd expected it to be easy. He felt such a connection to the music, but it was as a singer, not a musician. But he knew that it would help if he played an instrument. His father had finally given in and bought him a guitar. He knew it was out of guilt, but he was still glad to have it. He hadn't blinked an eye either when Cole told him he'd be picking up the tab for lessons, too. It had felt like a win at the time, but now he wasn't so sure.

"Just keep at it. The guitar is one of the more complicated instruments to learn," his instructor, said. Ernie was retired and supplemented his income by giving lessons. Cole knew that he had been a great player in his time and had been in a local band for years.

"Thanks. I'll get it eventually," Cole said.

"Sure you will. Just keep at it."

Cole practiced whenever he had a chance. He had a love/hate relationship with his guitar. He knew if he could at least get comfortable with it, he'd be able to compete with the other up and comers. But, it wasn't easy. At least he had his voice. Whenever he went to an open mic or karaoke nights with friends, he always got up, and everyone raved about his singing. They said it was something special. Especially the girls he dated.

"You should go to Nashville, or go on the Voice. You could totally win," Brandy, his latest date, had gushed after their last outing. She was a sweet girl, and Cole appreciated her support. He just wished it was Laura sitting beside him. He still couldn't get past that, missing her. He thought of her often. She was always the first person he wanted to call when something good happened, and it still hurt that it wasn't possible.

Cole was still barely speaking to his father, but he was starting to thaw a little as his father was trying really hard. First the guitar and the lessons, and recently he invited him to a dinner at the club to meet a new woman he was dating. He seemed nervous to have his blessing and Cole was flattered that he cared. And he was impressed with his date. Claire was a few years younger than his father, but he liked her immediately. She was attractive and friendly, and had an interesting career of her own. She was a veterinarian and had a local practice that specialized in cats. She also had two sons in middle school and was a widow. She seemed really nice and he'd never seen his father so happy. She seemed to soften him, somehow. He smiled a lot when he was around her and it was the kind of smile that reached his eyes. Cole was glad to see it. Even if it made him think of Laura and how that was how she'd always made him feel. It still confused him. How could he have been so wrong about her?

A FEW WEEKS after classes started, Cole decided to get some closure. He knew Laura was at the University of Montana and he bought himself an airline ticket and flew out there on a Thursday night, determined to find her whether it took a day or a week. As it turned out, he didn't have to wait long. He was roaming the campus grounds and was near the student center when he saw Laura walk out of the cafe. She was holding a stack of books and looked as beautiful as ever. He was about to walk over to her when he saw something that made him stop in his tracks. A tall, blonde student pulled Laura in for a hug and a kiss. She didn't protest, but rather sank into him and closed her eyes. Cole recognized the dreamy smile and it hit him like a gut punch. His father was right. Laura had moved on. And there was nothing left to talk about. He watched for a moment longer as the happy couple laughed and then strolled off in the opposite direction. Cole hailed a cab and went straight to the airport. His heart hurt, but he'd gotten what he needed. He knew that he'd be able to move on now.

LAURA SETTLED into college life easily and loved her time there. She and Tina had several classes together and she met Chris, a sweet and very handsome basketball player during her first week of classes and dated him for a little over a month, until he wanted to get serious. Laura enjoyed his company, but preferred to keep things light and focus on her classes and hanging out with her friends. She couldn't explain why she felt this why but the whole time she was dating Chris she felt oddly disloyal. It was a feeling that she couldn't seem to shake. She'd asked Aunt Helen if she'd been dating anyone before the accident, but she said no, that there hadn't been anyone special.

She dated a few others during her four years in college, but there was never anyone special, never anything that progressed to be serious. Laura kept busy with classes, and working at the music store too and in her spare time, she continued to dabble with writing songs and getting better at playing the guitar.

CHAPTER 7

It was a sunny Saturday afternoon in May and as usual, Laura was at the music shop, working her one weekly shift. She'd worked there every summer during college, and since graduating and taking a teaching job in Bozeman, she'd kept up the one day a week. Mostly because she loved playing music with Peter and running her new song ideas by him. She had a sizable stack of finished songs now and a dream of someday doing something with them. She enjoyed her job teaching music to elementary school children and spending Saturday afternoons at the shop. She knew her aunt enjoyed having her back home, too, especially since Harold had passed a year ago. It had been a difficult year for her, but she seemed to be doing much better now.

Laura had just finished playing her most recent song, which Peter pronounced her best yet, when the door opened with a whoosh and Tina flew in. She and Laura had quickly become best friends the first summer they worked together and had gone on to room together at college. She looked excited as she ran over to Peter and Laura.

"I got the job! Pack your bags, we're moving to Nashville in two weeks!"

"What? Are you serious?" Laura was excited for her friend but a wave of terror washed over her at the thought of moving. She had a nice, comfortable life in Bozeman. Could she really give that up to follow a pipe dream? She didn't want to perform—her goal was to sell her songs to others. She'd done plenty of research. Nashville was the place to go if you were serious about a career in country music. As much as Laura dreamed of it...the reality of moving was terrifying. It felt too sudden.

"You can't back out now. You promised. You know you need to go there. You're just scared," Tina said. They had an agreement at Tina's suggestion. If she got one of the marketing jobs she was applying for in Nashville, the two of them would move there together. Tina knew that Laura wasn't likely to go on her own.

Laura nodded. Her friend knew her well. She said nothing, just sat quietly trying to take it all in. Peter got her attention by grabbing her hand and looking at her intently.

"You have to go. Seriously. This is your chance. You have the talent and now you have the opportunity. I'll expect regular reports." He smiled and Laura recognized the truth in what he said. It was time.

Aunt Helen took the news well. Laura felt guilty leaving her alone, but her aunt brushed her concern aside.

"Honey, don't worry about me. I'll be fine. It's getting easier every day. I'm starting to do more on the weekends, too, catching up with friends. I have plenty to keep me busy." That was true. Since Harold's death, her aunt had her whole weekends to herself now and had recently started to go out more. She'd joined a women's knitting group that met on Saturday afternoons. She'd had made some new friends there and was getting more involved at her church as well. Laura relaxed as it seemed that her aunt was genuinely excited for her.

"I've heard you playing that guitar for hours and heard you singing. I know you don't like the attention, but you have a gift, honey. You could perform, you know?"

Laura shook her head. "The thought of that terrifies me. To get up in front of people and sing. No, I'm not looking to do that. But, I'd love to see if I can sell some of my songs."

"Your songs are wonderful. I'm sure you'll be able to do that." She looked thoughtful for a moment and then asked. "Do all singers write songs, too?"

"No, though a lot do. I've read that there is always a demand for new songs. I guess I'll find out." Laura grinned and her aunt pulled her in for a tight hug.

"I'm thrilled for you, though I'll miss you, of course. You'll come home for the holidays, right?"

Laura smiled. "Of course."

COLE WAS ENJOYING law school more than he would ever admit to his father. He'd just finished his first year. He and his father had worked out a deal. He agreed to get his law degree and, in return, his father paid for it and also agreed to let him go off to Nashville when he graduated and follow his dream. His father was sure it would only be for a year or two, but the agreement was however long it took and when Cole was ready, there would be a spot for him in his father's company. There was also a trust fund that he would have access to upon graduation, which would be helpful for expenses in Nashville.

His father was the governor now and from all accounts, was doing a great job. The economy in Charleston had improved and he'd just been voted in for a second term. His father also approved of his latest girlfriend. Chelsea was the daughter of one of his good friends, and Cole knew that his father would love for him to settle down with her and give up the pipe dream of Nashville. He had to admit, Chelsea was an intriguing girl. She was unlike anyone that he'd dated before.

She looked like the rest. She was a pretty sorority girl with long blonde hair, blue eyes and a killer smile, but she was also ambitious. She was impressed with Cole's father and admitted that she had political ambitions herself. When he shared that with his father one night at dinner, he lit up and a week later had arranged for a prestigious summer internship for Chelsea in the governor's public relations office.

"Your father is such an amazing man!" she'd gushed when they had dinner together a week after she started. They were at the country club, and it was a gorgeous Saturday night in late June. Warm breezes wafted over them as they sat outside on the veranda sipping gin and tonics.

"I'm glad you like it there." He'd never seen her this excited before. Chelsea was positively glowing as she told him all about her first week and all the important people she'd come in contact with.

"It's an incredible networking opportunity. This could lead to something wonderful."

"I'm sure it will." He smiled and took a sip of his drink. And then he shared his big news.

"We got our first gig. Me and the guys. We're going to play a set at Rusty's Lounge in two weeks."

Cole had been at a local karaoke night over the summer and at the end of the night, he'd been approached by three guys his age that were putting together a band and needed a singer. He started practicing with them that week.

Chelsea pursed her lips as if she'd tasted something particularly sour or distasteful, which wasn't exactly the reaction he'd been hoping for.

"Rusty's Lounge? Really? That place is a dive."

She did have a point there.

"Well, yeah. But they pack them in and they're paying us!"

Chelsea smiled and lifted her drink, "Well, congrats then!"

"Thanks. So you'll come watch us? Get some of your friends together?"

Chelsea was non-committal. "We'll see. I'll try."

Cole knew that meant chances were slim to none that she'd be there. But that was okay. He knew she hated country music and her friends weren't fond of it, either. But fortunately, plenty of other people were and he looked forward to playing for them soon.

CHAPTER 8

Nashville was everything Laura had imagined it would be, and more. There was an energy to the city that welcomed and inspired her. She and Tina found a modest, two-bedroom apartment in a less expensive area. The realtor had suggested it once Laura told her she was looking to build a career in music.

"You definitely want to be in that neighborhood. It's one of the most artsy areas, affordable, too."

They drove into town on a Friday, spent the weekend unpacking and exploring, and then Tina started her new job as a marketing coordinator for a software company on Monday. She'd held a similar role with a tech company in Bozeman, so it seemed like a good fit. After she left for work, Laura showered and changed, grabbed her notebook and walked up the street to a small coffee shop she'd noticed when they moved in. She bought a newspaper at the counter, ordered a frothy cappuccino and then settled at a small table next to a window that looked out over the street. It was a Monday morning and fairly quiet except for a few scattered people hunched over their laptops.

Laura opened the newspaper and found what she was looking for near the end. There was a listing of all the open mic and writer's nights for the week. Laura wanted to hit as many of them as possible. Just to listen and observe and learn the lay of the land. From her research, she'd learned that several places were known for their open mic or writer's nights when only original new songs were performed. Eventually, maybe she would get the courage to get up there herself. She knew that a necessary evil of selling a song was demonstrating it and that meant singing in front of people. The thought filled her with fear, but also a strange excitement, too, at the possibility of people hearing her music, her words. Even if they were stuck hearing her voice. At least she knew she had the ability to sing on key, which was a good thing. As long as she didn't freeze up and forget the words, she shouldn't embarrass herself too badly.

She folded the paper up and opened her notebook. A new song had come to her, and she had the music down but was still struggling to find the right words. It was another song about love lost, which never failed to amuse Tina.

She had heard her working on the song the night before and had asked, "Where does all of that come from? As far as I know, you've never had any bitter breakups. Dan even wished you well when we left."

Dan was the most recent guy that Laura had dated. They'd gone out for a few months, but as she always did,

Laura had told him that she wasn't looking to get serious and they'd kept things light. She considered him a good friend.

"I don't know where it comes from," Laura answered honestly. "It's just there. It's what comes to me. I think it's just from observing life around me."

Tina raised her eyebrow. "Maybe. Or maybe you have a secret history that would shock us all," she teased. Tina was one of the few people that Laura had confided in about the accident and what she now accepted as permanent amnesia.

"I doubt that. I was just a kid," she'd replied.

She spent the next half-hour lost in her inner world of melodies and words.

"You look deep in thought. Songwriter? Or novelist?" The deep voice to her right startled her out of her thoughts, and she jumped.

"Sorry, hope I didn't interrupt?" Laura glanced up and saw a smiling, dark-haired man who looked about her age.

"Trying to write a song," she admitted.

"I'm Jason. Are you new around here?" He held out his hand, and she shook it.

"Laura. We just moved in up the street this past weekend."

"In the gray building?"

Laura nodded.

"I'm right across the street. Also new to the area and an aspiring country music artist."

"You write songs, too?"

Jason chuckled. "Me and everyone else in town, it seems. Mind if I join you?"

"Sure."

He pulled out a chair, and the next hour flew as they chatted about music and their dreams. Jason was from Boston and had gone to a respected music college, Berklee. He also shared her fear of performing.

"It's a necessary evil. I'm sort of used to it now. There was a group of us that used to go to open mic nights around Cambridge and Boston. My songs are better than my voice."

"Same here," Laura admitted and then asked, "Did any of your college friends come here with you?"

"One did. Rufus was the only one in our group who was into country music."

"Is he a songwriter, too?"

"Not as much. He's more into playing the music, and his real love is the blues. We're trying to put a band together. So far it's just him and me, but eventually, it will be focusing on bluesy country." Jason grinned. "I play a mean harmonica."

Laura laughed and felt happy that she seemed to have made her first friend in Nashville. "I bet you do."

"So, let's hit some writer nights this week. I'll take you to my favorite spots."

"I'd love that. Those are open mic nights?"

"Yes, for showcasing songwriting, original new music only. We have to go early, though, to have a chance to go on."

"Oh, I'm not ready to go on yet. I was planning to just go and listen for a while."

Jason looked at her intently. "All right. This week you observe. But you need to dive in sooner rather than later... first time is the hardest, I promise."

"All right. Next week, maybe I'll do it."

"First one is tonight. Rufus and I will be by to get you at seven. We have to be there by eight at the latest."

"Great. I'll bring Tina, my roommate."

Tina didn't care that it was a Monday night. She was thrilled to go out and was excited about her first day on the new job. Laura poured them both a small glass of white wine, and they celebrated a successful first day by sitting on their tiny deck and watching the traffic go by below.

"The company seems great so far. Everyone is so friendly, and it's a casual environment. I was a little overdressed, but that's better than being underdressed. The girls are more done up here though—bigger hair, more makeup, nice though."

"Well, that's the South for you," Laura said automatically, and Tina looked at her curiously.

"You sounded as if you were speaking from experience. Did you ever live in the South? Or know people who did?"

Laura felt her head start to throb and pressed her hand against her forehead. The pain eased up after a minute, and she looked at Tina in confusion.

"What did you ask me?"

"It was nothing. Are you feeling all right?" She sounded worried, and Laura smiled. She took a sip of her wine.

"I'm fine. Just a headache for a minute there. It's gone now."

"So, tell me about this Jason. You said he has a friend?"

"Yes. I haven't met him yet, though." She told her all about Jason and their plans to go to a writer's night.

"Should you bring your guitar?" Tina asked.

"No, not tonight. I'm just listening, getting familiar with how these places operate. Then maybe I'll work up the courage eventually to get up there."

"Not eventually," Tina said with a frown.

"I know. I promised Jason I'd just watch this week. Next week it's my turn. Though I'll admit the thought of it terrifies me."

"You'll be fine. Better than fine. I have no doubt." Tina sounded so sure of it that Laura relaxed a little. She was grateful for her support.

Just as they finished their wine, there was a knock at the door. They grabbed their purses and Laura opened the door. She introduced Tina to Jason, and he introduced his roommate Rufus to the two of them. Laura liked Rufus instantly. He was a tall, gangly guy with reddish brown hair and freckles. He was cute though, too, with blue eyes and a great smile. His eyes lit up when Laura introduced him to Tina, and the four of them piled into Jason's Jeep and headed off to the Commodore Grill. Jason explained that the open mic part of the night didn't start until ten, but they'd hear great music before that.

"Tomorrow night we have to go to Douglas Corner café. That's my favorite of the bunch. It's a little earlier there. The first performer goes on at eight."

"Why is it your favorite?" Laura asked.

"The whole night is focused on original, new music. It's the ultimate writer's night."

When they made their way into the Commodore Grill, it was already packed. They put their names in for a table and then had a drink at the crowded bar. Soon after, they were seated and given dinner menus.

"The food here is pretty good. Killer nachos," Jason said.

They all decided to get burgers and share an order of nachos. The burgers were great, and the scheduled bands were impressive as well. Laura enjoyed all of them, from a classic country to more pop and even a bluegrass band. There was a short break between the last band and the open mic portion of the night, and then the host announced the first performer.

A skinny, young man wearing jeans, a white t-shirt, and a well-worn cowboy hat made his way up on to the stage. He had a guitar with him and looked nervously at the crowd as he slipped the strap over his shoulder. He waited a moment for the room to quiet down and then he started to play. Tentatively at first, then with more confidence as he started to sing. His voice was raspy and rich, and Laura was immediately captivated by his soulful sound. He sang a song of love lost that she connected to somehow. She loved every bit of it and was the first to clap when he finished.

"He was amazing," she said to the group.

"Richie is good. I've seen him play at a bunch of the open mic nights lately. That's one of his better songs."

They weren't all good, though. The first two were great, and Laura was starting to feel intimidated. No wonder Nashville was referred to as Music City. Just as her self-doubt was mounting, a new performer came on, and he was awful. So bad that she looked at the others and raised her eyebrows.

"There's always a few clunkers. I find it reassuring that they're not all great," Jason said with a grin. He understood completely. Laura missed the name of the next performer, but Jason gave her wrist a squeeze as he stood and said, "Wish me luck." He grabbed his guitar and made his way to the front of the room.

Laura sat back and waited, excited to hear how her new friend would sound. She was a little nervous too, hoping that he'd be significantly better than the one they'd just heard.

He was.

His voice was deceptively soft at first, and Laura leaned forward in her seat a bit to hear. But then he moved into the heart of his song, and she felt goosebumps. He was that good. She wasn't sure if it was his voice or his lyrics, but the combination of the bluesy sound and the melody was compelling. Jason was a charismatic performer. He had that certain quality that some performers have where you are spellbound while they are on stage. The applause came loud and fast when he finished, and as he walked back to their table, several people high-fived him. He smiled shyly as he sat back in his chair and settled his guitar beside him.

"That was amazing, really wonderful," Laura said happily. Jason looked relieved.

"Thank you. I was hoping you'd like it."

"Rufus, are you going up, too?" Laura asked. He looked startled by the question, then grinned.

"No. I chickened out tonight. Still fine-tuning something. It's not ready yet."

"He is a wimp," Jason confirmed. "I've heard what he has so far, and it's pretty great."

"Will you play it for us soon?" Tina asked.

"Maybe next week," Rufus said, and Laura watched with interest as a red flush spread across his face when Tina smiled at him. Laura was happy to see that he and Tina seemed to be hitting it off. They'd been chatting easily all night. Jason and Rufus were both really nice guys, and Laura was glad they'd met some people their age already.

Around eleven thirty they left. When Jason dropped them off, he confirmed that they were both ready to do it again the next night.

"Looking forward to it," Laura agreed as she and Tina climbed out of the Jeep and waved as they drove off.

CHAPTER 9

L aura's first week in Nashville was a good one. They'd gone to several more open mic nights, and on Saturday night, they joined Jason and Rufus and a few more of their friends for a pub crawl. They went to five different clubs and listened to music of all sorts until the wee hours. Laura was having the time of her life, and when she phoned home on Sunday, her aunt commented on how happy she sounded.

"Well, I can see that I've been worried for nothing. You sound wonderful, honey."

Laura let her know how her job search was progressing. "I've applied to a bunch of schools in the area, just to have my resume on file. There was only one music teacher opening, so I'm not going to hold my breath on that. But, I also put my name in to be a sub, so I should be able to at least get some part-time work once the school year starts.

"And you're still drawing salary through the summer," her aunt said. Laura had elected to be paid yearly so she would still be collecting a check for most of the summer, which was a relief. She had some money saved too as her expenses had been minimal this past year while she lived at home. Her aunt filled her in on all the people she knew and mentioned that she'd run into Peter at the supermarket.

"He asked me if you'd sung anywhere yet in Nashville? Made me promise to ask you. What's that all about?"

Laura chuckled. "He knows me so well. If you see him again, tell him yes. I watched this week, but I promised a friend I'd do it this coming Tuesday."

"You'll do great, honey. Good luck!"

Laura hung up and felt a flash of homesickness, but it only lasted a minute. She missed her aunt, as she was the only family she had, but she was very glad to be in Nashville. It felt like home already, and she knew it was where she was supposed to be.

It had been a good writing week too, the most productive week that she'd ever had. Once Tina left for work in the morning, Laura had fallen into a routine of walking to the little coffee shop on the corner, reading the paper while she drank her coffee, and then opening her notebook and writing down all the random ideas that came to mind. Sometimes it was a struggle to get more than a few words down. Other times, they came so fast and furious that she wrote as quickly as she could to keep up and get it all down. Sometimes she'd run into Jason, and he confessed that his routine was similar. They'd walk back together, and Laura would grab her guitar and settle on the living room sofa, her notebook by her side. She would play for hours, fine-tuning until the music in her head wrapped around the right words in a way that pleased her. Sometimes it all came together easily, but most days the right combination was elusive, coming close but not quite right. She kept at it, though, sometimes working on the same song for several days until it clicked and the magic happened. It didn't always, though. She had more not quite done songs than ones she was happy with. But it always gave her things to work on.

"Are you nervous for tonight?" Jason asked on Tuesday as they walked home after getting coffee.

"I've never done this before, you know," she admitted. "What if I can't do it?"

That was her biggest fear. That she'd get up in front of a crowd of people, open her mouth and nothing would come out.

Jason stopped walking and stared at her. "Are you saying you've never sung anywhere? Ever?"

Laura nodded. "Just in the music shop, for Peter, the owner. He's the one that taught me to play. And encouraged me to come here."

"So he believes in you."

"He does. He asked my aunt if I'd done it yet and I told her to tell him it would happen this week. So, I have to do it. But I'm terrified."

"Well, I'm not going to lie to you and tell you it's easy or that you'll do great. I hope you will, but don't worry if nerves get the best of you. My first time up wasn't pretty."

"No? What happened?" Laura was intrigued. Jason seemed so confident and experienced. It was hard to imagine him being nervous on stage.

"I made the mistake of looking at the audience too soon before I was comfortable with how I'd started. When I saw a room full of people all staring at me, I lost it. My voice cracked, and I forgot half the words. It was all I could do to finish and then slink back to my table."

"That's exactly what I picture happening," Laura admitted.

"Expect the worst, and it won't be so bad. It got better from there, the more I did it. You just have to keep showing up. It's a nice crowd mostly. Even if you bomb, they'll appreciate that you got up there and tried."

"Okay. That's all I can do I guess, just try?"

Jason grinned. "That's what I tell myself each week. I still get nervous. But it's a great way to try out new songs and see how people react. They'll get to know you, too, and that's what it's all about."

"Well, I guess I'm as ready as I'll ever be. Might as well get the first time over with."

"I really do think you'll do just fine...even though I haven't heard a note yet. I have a good feeling about you."

Laura smiled. "I hope I won't let you down then..."

LAURA COULD BARELY EAT for the rest of the day. She was far too nervous. She kept tinkering with one of the songs she was planning to play. It was a variation of the first song she'd ever written. Peter had told her that it was special and over the years, she kept revisiting it. Of all her songs, it was the one that felt the most personal somehow, yet she couldn't explain why. She just knew how it made her feel—sad, but somehow hopeful at the same time as the song spoke about losing and then finding love again. It felt like the right song for her to sing. And at least she knew that it wasn't possible for her to forget the words. They were ingrained in her soul at this point. She'd be singing two songs and hadn't decided about the other one but thought it might be one of the newer ones she'd been working on.

She spent an hour trying to decide what to wear, putting on one combination after another and rejecting them all. Tina walked into her room when she got home from work and laughed at her.

"What on earth are you doing?"

"I have nothing to wear..." Laura said miserably as she stared at her closet and the various pieces of clothing that she'd flung across her bed.

Tina stared at her for a moment, thinking hard. Then she went to her closet, rummaged through it until she found what she was looking for and handed Laura a top that she'd overlooked. It was deceptively simple, a soft buttery suede halter style in a caramel shade that flattered her long blonde hair. Tina then picked up a faded pair of jeans that she'd already discarded and tossed them at her.

"That with those jeans and your brown cowboy boots. Done."

Laura laughed. "Okay, fine. I'll be ready in five minutes, then."

And she was. She felt good about what she was wearing. The jeans were comfortable and flattering, and she liked the way the sleeveless top made her arms look. Jason apparently agreed as he whistled with appreciation when he and Rufus came to collect them.

"You look great!"

LAURA GRABBED HER GUITAR, and they headed out. The place was already busy when they arrived, and they were lucky to get the last available table. Laura had done as Jason had instructed and called a few minutes before one to get her name on the list to perform. She was on the list but wasn't sure what time she would be called up. It could be anytime, and they played as late as one. She enjoyed hearing the different artists perform, but it was impossible to relax, and each time they called a different name, she jumped. Jason was called first, and then Rufus. It was her first time hearing Rufus play, and she enjoyed both of his songs. They had a mournful, soulful sound that seemed a little at odds with his bright red hair and freckles, but after a moment that didn't matter as she lost herself in the music. Jason had a good night, too, and the crowd warmly applauded for both of them. Finally, a few minutes past ten, Laura's name was called.

She rose nervously as Jason handed her her guitar and smiled encouragingly. The walk to the stage seemed to take forever. Finally, she was in front of the mic, and once she had her guitar in place, she took a deep breath and started to play. The sound relaxed her, and she forced herself not to look at the audience, but to glance instead toward her table, to find a focal point. Her eyes met Jason's, and then she smiled and started to sing. Her voice was shaky at first, through the first half of the song, as her nerves got the best of her. She knew the music sounded fine, but she was too aware of everything to lose herself in the words like she usually did and she knew it wasn't her best effort. It frustrated her that her voice was so wobbly.

When she finished the song, there was polite applause, and Jason gave her the thumbs up. She knew she hadn't wowed anyone, but at least she hadn't forgotten the words. She started strumming again and felt a bit more relaxed as she started to sing what she thought of as her best song. Her voice was stronger now, and she felt the energy around her shift as the audience seemed to collectively lean forward. She closed her eyes and lost herself in the emotion of the song, digging deep to tell it the way it needed to be told. Her voice cracked and grew a bit raspy as it always seemed to do as she reached the end of the song, but she knew that it worked, too. When she opened her eyes and stopped singing, the room was silent and then erupted in enthusiastic clapping. Her eyes found Jason, and he was beaming. A sense of relief washed over her. She knew the first song had been rough, but she'd done her best on the second, and it seemed to have gone over well enough. She picked up her guitar, made her way back to the table and was surprised to be stopped several times along the way as people told her she did a great job and introduced themselves. Most of the names went in one ear and out the other, but she was happy to meet them all and to shake hands with everyone.

When she reached the table, Jason pulled out her chair and gave her a hug before she sat down.

"You did great!" Tina said. "I've heard you sing before, but that was amazing."

"Nice job," Rufus agreed.

"The first song was a little rocky," Jason began, and Laura nodded. "But you crushed it on that second one. Totally different feel. That was really special." He looked pleased, a little surprised even, and Laura recognized something else in his eyes—respect. Tina and Rufus were deep in conversation again, and Jason leaned over and said, "You're good you know. Really good. Those people who stopped you and introduced themselves? They knew it, too. You need to start doing this regularly now, get known, then doors will start to open for you."

"You really think so?" Laura's head was spinning.

Jason chuckled. "I know so. If there's more where that came from?"

Laura thought of the piles of songs stacked along the floor of her bedroom and grinned.

"There's more!"

CHAPTER 10

Rusty's Lounge really was a dive. The smell of stale beer assaulted his senses when Cole and the other guys in the band arrived to set up for their first performance together. It was early still, just half-past six, and there were only a handful of guys there, drinking draft beer at the bar.

Rusty's looked like it had been built in a weekend by people who didn't really know what they were doing. There were visible cracks in the windows, dangling light fixtures over the two well-worn pool tables, slanted, dirty floors and mismatched bar stools. Cole was relieved now that Chelsea wouldn't be there. She'd called earlier to say she'd forgotten that she'd promised to go somewhere with her mother. Cole wasn't entirely sure that he believed her, but he knew she'd hate it at Rusty's, so it was for the best.

The customers at the bar were mostly older men, still in their various work uniforms. Cole guessed that they'd stopped by for an after-work beer or three and probably wouldn't be staying to hear the band play. They were friendly enough, though. Once they were set up, Cole and the guys went to the bar and had a beer as well. The older men were on their way out, settling their tabs and heading home for the night.

"Sorry I can't stick around to hear you boys play," one of them said as he stood to leave. "The missus wouldn't like it. Good luck. Susie, I'll see you tomorrow."

"Bye, Gerry!" the cheerful bartender, a cute college girl, called out as he and his friends left together.

"Think it will pick up soon?" Cole asked.

Susie chuckled. "Just wait. An hour from now, this place will be packed again. It's like they change shifts. The daytime guys go home and then the students come in."

It was hard to imagine, but within a half hour, people started streaming in and as Susie had predicted, the place was soon packed and it was time for them to go on.

They headed to the corner where they had everything set up and started to warm up. Cole was excited and nervous. He had his guitar strapped on but it was mostly for show. The guys had assured him that they had the playing covered so all he had to do was strum a little and focus on singing. Which was just as he liked it. They were mostly going to do covers of all the popular artists that were climbing the charts and a few classics, too, like Johnny Cash. The owner of the bar had told them not to play too many original songs. Said his crowd liked to hear songs they knew. That was fine with Cole. He just liked to sing, period. But he was also excited to do several of the new songs the guys in the band had written. Toby was the true songwriter of the bunch and a strong guitarist, but his voice was admittedly weak. Which is why they recruited Cole.

They started with a lively song that was zooming up the charts, a Blake Shelton tune that everyone was familiar with. The song fit Cole's voice perfectly. The slight twinge of nerves disappeared as soon as he started to sing and the music and energy of the crowd surrounded him. He relaxed and put his personality into it and had fun with the song. He could tell by the way people had stopped talking and were paying attention that they were liking it. When he finished, there was a huge round of applause. He noticed with amusement that several groups of girls had resettled themselves closer to the band and were alternating between staring at him and giggling amongst themselves.

"They like you. Nice job!" Toby said as they moved into their next song. After about an hour, they did an original song, and it went over well, too. They took a break after that and Toby went to the bar to get them a round of beers. When he came back, two cute blonde girls were with him. Toby handed out the beers to Cole and the other two guys in the band, and then introduced the girls.

"They wanted to meet you. Cole, this is Stacey and Kathryn." He wandered off to chat with one of the guys and left Cole alone with the girls.

"We loved your singing. Your voice is awesome!" Stacey said.

"Really great. Are you going to do this for real?" Kathryn asked. She was cute. They both were.

"For real?" Cole teased.

"I mean, are we going to be able to buy your CDs one day? Will we hear you on the radio?"

"That would be pretty cool. Would you buy my CD if I made one?"

"Yes!" they both said at the same time.

"Well, that sure is nice to hear. Thank you. I think we're going to start playing in a minute or two, so I have to go check in with the guys. Enjoy the rest of your night!"

Cole was still smiling as he walked over to the guys who were sitting around a small table next to the equipment.

"You have fans already," Toby said.

"They were sweet. Said if we made a CD, they'd buy it. Imagine that?"

The guys exchanged glances.

"We were going to wait and see how things went with you, but we were just talking and getting a CD made is something we want to do. We just needed to get the right vocalist to bring it all together." He paused and then asked, "How serious are you about making music? Is this just something you're playing with while you're in school?"

Cole felt three sets of eyes staring at him, waiting for his response. They didn't have to wait long.

"This is it, man. It's what I want to do. Always has been. Law school is for my father."

"So you'll be able to play nights, weekends, whenever we can get a gig lined up?" Toby questioned.

Cole grinned. "I'm in. You book it and I'm there."

CHAPTER 11

ONE YEAR LATER...

The engagement party for Tina and Rufus was a surprise. Laura had carefully set it up so that they thought it was just another writer's night out. A typical Tuesday at the Douglas Cafe. They were regulars now and Laura had given a few of their friends the heads up so they'd be sure to be there. Tina quickly figured out that something was up when they were led to an unusually large table, reserved for their group of ten—Jason, Rufus, Tina, Laura and the small group of friends they'd made during the past year. There was a cake in the middle of the table, and balloons tied to the edge of the platter. In shiny red frosting, the message on the cake read, "Congratulations on your engagement, Tina and Rufus!"

"I can't believe you did this!" Tina pulled Laura in for a quick hug, while Rufus looked embarrassed. "Thank you."

They settled in around the table, and their friends joined them soon after and more congratulations were shared. Laura was glad to see her friend so happy. Tina and Rufus had hit it off immediately and had been together since. They were opposites, with Tina being the bubbly, outgoing one and Rufus the quieter, more reserved one.

"Have you set a date yet?" Connie, one of their friends, asked.

"We're not in a hurry. Probably a year or so from now. We want to save money, so we'll have a nice down payment and can buy something. Plus, I'm not ready to give up the single life just yet!"

"I'd miss you too much," Laura added. It was true. Even though Tina spent half her time staying at Rufus's place, she was home enough and Laura knew she'd miss her fun energy. Whenever Tina was there, they were always doing something fun, and she went to almost every writer's night with them. Laura's own love life was lackluster. She and Jason had flirted initially with the idea of dating but quickly settled into a more comfortable friendship.

He was dating someone pretty seriously now, and Laura liked her quite a bit. She'd actually introduced the two of them, as Janet was a fellow teacher at the elementary school where Laura had landed a permanent job after six months of substitute teaching. When the music teacher had retired, Laura was there as the obvious replacement. She'd dated here and there, but there was no one so far that she'd fallen for. She wondered if she ever would.

"Are you excited for tomorrow?" Tina was sitting next

to her, and no one was paying attention when she asked the question. Laura hadn't said anything to anyone else yet, just Tina. There was too much at stake, and she didn't want to get her hopes up—again. Over the past year, she'd met a lot of people. Most of them had encouraged her, but some had also warned that it was really tough out there for songwriters who didn't want to perform. The bar was also very high, which Laura had realized after going to her first few writer's nights.

She knew she had the talent, and some of her songs were pretty good, but they weren't at the level they would need to be to be taken seriously by a major producer or record label. She wasn't discouraged, though. If anything, she was inspired by the talented people she was surrounded by. She listened and she learned. And when she was done teaching for the day and all her lesson planning was done, she wrote, and she played. Every day, without fail. She looked forward to it. It was as necessary as breathing.

Two days ago, when Tina had gotten home from work, she stopped short when she saw Laura, sitting Indian-style on the living room sofa, her guitar nowhere in sight.

"What's wrong?," she'd asked. "Where's your guitar? You're always playing when I walk through the door."

Laura had looked up in a daze. She was holding a piece of paper. "I got an email from Black Duck studios today. They liked my demo tape and want me to come in and meet with them. I printed it out and have been staring at it ever since, trying to convince myself that it's real."

"Yahoo!" Tina had squealed and rushed over to give

her a hug. "Of course it's real, silly. This is what you've been waiting for. Let me see." Laura handed her the sheet of paper and she read it out loud.

"Hi Laura, thanks for sending the tape. We liked it. Can you come in Wednesday afternoon to discuss possibly working together?"

"I'm not even sure what that means," Laura said.

"It means they like you. Maybe they want to buy one of your songs? How great would that be?"

"That would be incredible, and amazing. A dream come true."

Laura snapped her attention back to Tina's question.

"Yes, I'm excited. I doubt that I'll sleep much tonight."

"You'll do great. Have you talked to Lily by any chance? I missed a call from her earlier."

"I had a call from her earlier too. She just sold one of her songs to Anvil Records. Someone heard me sing it when she was here visiting us." They'd both gone to college with Lily and now she worked as an event planner Rivers End Resort in Idaho and wrote songs on the side.

"That's fantastic news! If it happened for her, it can happen to you too."

"I hope so."

"So, what are you going to wear?" Tina asked seriously.

Laura laughed. "I have no idea. You'll have to pick something out for me."

"I can do that."

Laura looked around the table at her friends. Rufus had gotten a full-time job with a local software company as a QA engineer. He'd given up on doing music full-time, but had hooked up with a few other guys and played in a band with them every now and then.

Jason was still determined. He'd gotten a job too, though, bartending a few shifts a week, mostly during the day so he'd have his nights free to play. Laura knew that he'd had a few meetings with different people he'd been referred to, but nothing had really come of it. Laura wasn't sure why. She liked his music and thought he had a smooth voice. She'd been in town long enough now though to know that it was an extremely competitive business. Every week a new batch of starry-eyed singer-songwriters rolled into town, convinced that they were going to be the next big thing.

They had been told that over and over again by others in their small towns or cities where they'd been a big fish in a small pond. But Nashville was the ocean and they were mere minnows, as they all quickly learned. During the last year, Laura had seen a number of the newcomers give up after a few months and move home, completely disillusioned. Others, like Jason and herself, were more patient. Jason had told her more than once that it could take years to get noticed. She wasn't in a hurry, either. She knew that her songs now were vastly improved from what she was able to do a year ago.

A few months ago, David, an artist she'd met at one of the writer's nights, had offered to help her put a demo tape together. He supported himself by doing voice-overs and narrating audiobooks and had a mini-studio in his house. Over several Sunday sessions, they managed to put together a tape of four of her best songs, including her favorite, the very first one she wrote, that had been revised so many times by now that she'd lost count. But she knew that it kept getting better and was one of her strongest songs.

Something kept her from saying anything to Jason about the meeting. She felt a little guilty because he was here first. Though she knew that was silly, and he'd probably be thrilled for her. She decided to tell him tonight as she realized he might be more upset if he heard about it after the fact. And maybe he'd have some words of wisdom for her.

An hour or so later, when the bands took a break and they were able to talk easily, she told him her news. A range of emotions flashed across his face—initially surprise, something she couldn't read, and then happiness.

"That's really great news. I knew it would happen for you, eventually. And Black Duck? That's impressive." Black Duck was an up-and-coming label that was producing some of the newest stars in Country music.

"I know. I had to print out the email to convince myself it was real."

He laughed at that. "I probably would have done the same thing."

"So, what will happen when I go in there? What should I expect?"

Jason thought for a minute. "It really depends what

they are thinking. If they see you as a songwriter to work with some of their existing artists, or if they want you to perform."

Laura frowned. "I made it clear when I sent in the tape that I was looking to write and sell songs. Not perform."

"Oh, all right, then. I'm sure that's what they want to discuss then, and to find out what else you are working on."

Laura relaxed and took a sip of her beer. "Good. That I can talk about. My stack of songs is taking over my bedroom."

At a quarter to four the following Wednesday afternoon, Laura drove her faded blue Honda Civic into the parking lot of Black Duck studios. Her heart raced as she grabbed her purse, keys and got out of the car. She did a last-minute check of her outfit and brushed a stray piece of lint off her gray dress pants. She'd been tempted to wear jeans, but that didn't feel appropriate for a business meeting. Yet, she didn't want to overdress either.

She finally settled on the pants she'd worn to work that day and changed into a flattering, pale blue lightweight sweater set, a simple shell with a cardigan over it. She laughed to herself as she realized it made her look exactly like what she was, an elementary school teacher. But, she hoped that her music would speak for itself.

She walked through the front door, and the receptionist smiled when she saw her. She took in her outfit and then asked, "Are you here to interview for the administrative position?" Ugh. Maybe she should have worn jeans.

"No, I have a meeting at four with Harry Evans."

"Oh? And your name?"

"Laura Scott." She looked at the calendar and then nodded.

"Please have a seat, Miss Scott. I'll let Harry know that you're here."

Laura sat on the soft leather sofa and picked up a dog-eared copy of the Nashville Scene, the local paper that listed all the week's musical events. After about ten minutes, she was almost done reading it when the receptionist called her.

"Mr. Evans will see you now. First door on your right."

"Thank you." Laura made her way down the hall and lightly tapped on the door which was open a few inches.

"Come in," a voice called. Laura pushed open the door and stepped into the office. A bald man who looked to be in his early fifties sat behind a massive desk piled high with papers and large manila envelopes.

"Laura Scott?"

She nodded and he held out his hand. "Harry Evans. A pleasure to meet you." He saw her glance at the stack of manila envelopes and grinned. "Those are demo tapes that have come in just today, if you can believe it."

Laura wasn't sure what to say to that, but it was intimidating, to say the least, and reinforced how many people were trying to do the same thing that she was.

"I'm sorry I didn't come out to get you. I was just finishing up a call. I thought we'd go into the conference room and have you meet a few other people on the team." He led the way down the hall and Laura followed close behind, curious about who the others were and why she was meeting them.

He opened the door to the conference room and gestured for Laura to go first. She walked in and then stopped in her tracks when she saw five people gathered around a large conference table, waiting expectantly.

"Everyone, this is Laura Scott. Laura, this is the team." He introduced them then, one by one, and their names went in one ear and out the other. It was overwhelming to be meeting with so many people at once, and Laura felt very shy and intimidated. Especially when they began discussing her as if she wasn't there.

"The hair is good, a few more highlights could work," said Ian, a creative looking guy with bleached blonde, spiky hair, and thick black glasses.

"She's tinier than I remember, shorter too. I like the innocent look she has going on," a woman next to Ian said, and he nodded. Laura thought her name was Gail. She wasn't sure why either of them cared about her appearance, though.

"Laura, have a seat, please." He indicated one of the two empty seats at the head of the table and sat in the other.

"So, as you can see, they are already excited to work with you. I haven't seen you perform yet, but Ian, Gail and Billy have, and I trust them implicitly. And as I said, I liked what I heard." He leaned forward, steepled his hands and looked at her intently.

"I have a few questions for you first. How many songs do you have? What are you working on? And how badly do you want this?"

Laura smiled. Those were easy questions.

"Just over two hundred. Another twenty or so in various stages of creation and I want this very badly."

"Good. And the instruments I hear on the demo tape, is that all you?"

"Yes, just me and my guitar."

"You ever play with a band before? Other instruments?"

Laura frowned. "No, I—well, I just write. I'm not really a performer. That's not my goal."

He looked at her and then looked around the table. They were all smiling as if they'd heard a particularly funny private joke.

"Here's the thing. Your songs are good, really good, and we're definitely interested in having you work with some of our other artists, maybe even doing some co-writing. But, what we're most interested in is you. Having you perform your own music. You have a unique sound and the right look for what we think is going to be hot."

Laura hesitated. This was unexpected. Flattering, but frightening. She chose her words carefully.

"Thank you. That's very kind of you to say. Is the co-writing contingent on me performing, too?"

Harry looked around the table and saw that they were all in agreement. He nodded.

"Yes. I think you underestimate your ability, my dear. We all believe in you." He went on then to tell her what they had in mind and by the time she left, an hour later, her head was spinning. He'd presented her with a contract, too, that spelled out everything they discussed and the terms of their offer. Laura didn't have any basis for comparison, but it seemed like a generous one.

"Go home and sleep on this...then call me in the morning and tell me that you're on board. I'll be expecting your call." He paper-clipped his business card to the contract, folded it in half and handed it to her.

"Thank you. It was great to meet all of you." Laura looked around the room and they were all smiling and congratulating her. Harry walked her out and even the receptionist congratulated her. It felt completely surreal as Laura walked out of the building and then got in to her car to drive home. Goosebumps raced up her arm and she shivered, even though it was nearly eighty degrees out. Her whole world had changed, just like that. She knew if she agreed to this offer that nothing would ever be the same again.

CHAPTER 12

Tina was in the kitchen when Laura got home. She barely remembered the drive back. Her mind was elsewhere, replaying the scene in the conference room. It didn't seem real. Tina smiled when she saw her, then reached into the refrigerator and pulled out a bottle of champagne.

"So, how did it go? Are we ready to pop this?"

"Maybe. It went a little differently than I expected." Laura set her purse down and joined Tina in the kitchen.

"Is that good or bad? Do they want to buy any of your songs?"

"They might...but there's a catch. They like my songs and said I might be able to co-write with some of their other artists...but they want me to perform."

Tina's jaw dropped. "They do?! But, that's great! Isn't it?"

Laura bit her lip. "It's really flattering, but it's a lot to wrap my head around. Performing was never the goal."

"Well, you're going to say yes, right? This is it. This is your big opportunity. You're better than you think, you know. There's something unique about your sound."

Laura smiled. "That's what they said, too."

"Well, they know, right?" Tina tore the foil wrapper off the bottle of champagne, wrapped her hand around the top of it and twisted the bottle slowly until they heard the distinctive pop. "This news is definitely champagne worthy." She poured them each a frothy glass, and they took them out onto the deck and settled onto the plastic folding chairs they kept there.

"Huge congrats!" Tina tapped her glass against Laura's, and they both took a sip. The crisp, bubbly wine tasted wonderful. And as confusing as it was, Laura did feel like celebrating.

"Honestly, it's a no-brainer the way I see it. What do you have to lose? School just wrapped for the year. You have all summer to try this, and you seem much more comfortable on stage than you used to be."

"That's true. It is easier now." Laura wasn't nearly as nervous as she used to be when they called her to sing. She didn't mind it as much and once she started to sing, the nerves dissipated as she lost herself in the music. She wasn't sure if she was ready to be the focus of attention, though. She had always preferred to be in the background and the idea of having someone else sing one of her songs was so much more appealing. But they did say she could do that, too.

"It would be foolish to say no to this. I know that. I just need to sleep on it and get used to the idea."

"I'm excited for you! I think you'll do really great. Maybe you'll have your own band?"

Laura nodded. "They said they could help me with that, put together a backup band and get me some gigs with some of their other artists. Start small at first, open for them and just do a few songs."

"Imagine if you're the headline act someday? How crazy would that be? I can see it, though." Tina said proudly.

"You can? I can't. It's completely surreal to me. I almost feel guilty because so many people would kill for this chance and I'm scared to death."

"Think of the money potential," Tina said practically. "You'll make money on the CD and download sales, but the real money is in touring. Live shows."

"I've never thought much about the money. It's never been about that for me."

"I know it hasn't. Or you wouldn't be teaching. But, the reality is, you might not have to worry about it anymore."

"I can't even think about that."

"When do they want an answer?"

"I told him I'd call tomorrow morning."

"Well, we'll have to go out tomorrow night then, and celebrate for real!"

LAURA WOKE FEELING ODDLY calm and at peace. She

called Harry Evans at a few minutes past nine, and the receptionist put her right through.

"Are you calling me with good news?" He sounded as if he'd already had two cups of coffee and was full of energy and enthusiasm. Laura was only half-way into her first cup and barely awake, but she wanted to make the call before she lost her nerve.

"I am. I'm excited to work with you."

"Fantastic! Why don't you come on in next Monday, and we'll get things rolling for you? Do you have a manager?"

"Um, no."

"Okay, I know a good guy I can refer to you. If it's all right with you, I'll have him give you a call this week. He'll work with you to get your name out there more and get you some gigs, once you're ready for it."

"Oh, all right."

"Name is Ricky Carson. You'll like him. Welcome aboard, Laura."

"Thank you." Laura set the phone down. It was done. She grabbed a sweatshirt, her notebook and headed out to the coffee shop. She needed to walk and was hoping she might see Jason to share her news. She was dying to tell someone who would understand.

The shop was almost empty when she walked in. It was just past nine thirty, so most people were already at work. Laura ordered her usual cappuccino and settled at her favorite small table by the window.

She had a few sips, but her coffee mostly grew cold as she day-dreamed and scribbled ideas in her notebook. She was so into her thoughts that she didn't hear Jason come up next to her and jumped at the sound of a chair moving.

"Am I interrupting?" he asked as he sat across from her.

"No, not at all. I was just in my own world. You know how it is."

Jason smiled. "I do, indeed. He pulled out his own notebook and pen, and then asked, "So, tell me all about it. How did it go?"

Lauren put her pen down and leaned back in her chair.

"It was crazy. Different than I expected, but hopefully good." She filled him on her meeting and what they had in mind.

"Are you okay with that?" he asked.

"Performing? I think so. It's an incredible opportunity, right? I'd be crazy to say no."

"I couldn't say no. If they wanted to throw money at me and put me up in front of people, I wouldn't think twice about it." Jason grinned. "I'm thrilled for you. A little envious, I'll admit it. But really happy for you. That's awesome news."

"Thank you. You really think it could be a good thing?"

Jason was quiet for a moment and then nodded. "I do. I know you'd prefer to just write your songs and hand them over, but you have a nice voice. There's a breathy quality, a sweet raspiness to it that is kind of innocent and sexy at the same time." He grinned at her and then added, "You're not bad-looking, either. I can see why they'd want you."

Laura laughed. She was relieved that he thought she could do it. Jason's opinion was important to her.

"I have some news, too. Not as big as yours, but still pretty cool."

"What?"

"I got a call from Andrew Wyatt. He's seen me a few times at recent writer nights and wondered if I might be interested in playing with his band on a trial basis, to see how it goes."

"Andrew Wyatt? Why does his name sound familiar?" Laura couldn't place who he was.

"He's the lead singer for the Downtown Blues band."

"Oh! Wow. That is exciting news." Laura had heard them play a few times over the past year and was impressed.

Jason smiled. "It's starting to happen for us."

The next week was a whirlwind of activity, beginning with a phone call from Ricky Carson, the manager that Harry had mentioned. He wanted to meet up for coffee and Laura suggested the shop down the street. They met that Friday morning at ten. Laura arrived at a quarter to and brought her cappuccino to her usual table by the window. That way she could keep an eye out for him— though she had no idea what he looked like. His voice was deep and warm, and he described himself as average height and wearing a baseball cap to make up for the fact that he had no hair. She liked that he laughed at himself. At a few minutes before ten, she watched a man approach the front door that fit that description. He walked in, looked around, then saw her and smiled.

"You must be Laura." He held out his hand to introduce himself. "Ricky Carson."

"Nice to meet you."

"I see you have your coffee. Can I get you anything else?"

"No, I'm good, thanks."

He walked off and returned a few minutes later with a cup of steaming black coffee and sat down across from her.

"So, I understand this is going to be a big change for you? And a huge opportunity. You weren't planning to perform?"

"That wasn't the plan originally, no," she admitted.

"But you're okay with it now?" He watched her carefully. She nodded.

"I think so. I'm a little nervous, of course. But, it's gotten easier to get up there. Especially when they like the songs."

Ricky leaned back in his chair, crossed his legs and took a long, slow sip of coffee.

"I listened to your demo tape. It's very good. I can help you connect with the right people and start playing around town, get your name known. We need to get a band together to support you."

"Harry said the same thing."

"We spoke about it a little. He has some ideas, and I do too. We thought we'd see who might be interested and then have you play with a few of them. See if the synergy is there. I have one band in particular in mind that could be interesting. They just lost their lead singer a few weeks ago and are trying to regroup."

"What happened to their singer?" Laura hoped it wasn't anything too tragic.

"Pregnancy and a husband who accepted a job out-of-state. Her singing was a hobby in his eyes. Too bad, because she was pretty good."

"Oh, that's too bad." Laura couldn't imagine giving up her career like that.

"Maybe it was more of a hobby to her. Hard to say. But the guys took it pretty hard. I sent one of their demos over to Harry to take a listen. We should know more in a few days. So, tell me more about you. What does Laura Scott want?"

Laura thought about that for a moment. No one had ever come out and asked her that before.

"I want people to hear my songs, and hopefully, to like them. That's all I've ever wanted."

Ricky smiled. "Well, I can help you with that, at getting the word out. If you want me to?"

"I'd like that."

"So, Daddy says if we get married this fall, he'll give us the Plantation house." Chelsea was lying with her head in Cole's lap as he idly ran his hands through her hair. They'd just had a delicious dinner at the club and were lounging on the living room sofa in the townhouse Chelsea shared with her best friend, Missy.

"The Plantation house? Wow." Chelsea's family was wealthy, and her father often did business with Cole's father. They owned multiple holdings around Charleston, and the Plantation house was a beauty. It overlooked marshlands and was on several grassy acres. The house itself was old, but roomy and well-maintained. Gorgeous, actually. The only problem was the location.

"So, should I tell him we accept?" Chelsea smiled up at him.

"Honey, that's generous of your father and very tempting, but you know I really need to go to Nashville," he said. `

"Well, I was thinking about that. You still have a year left in school, and this is where all of our family and friends are and my best chances for a job after graduation. If we marry in the fall and move into the Plantation, you'll have a home base. Then when you graduate, you can go to Nashville every now and then. You don't have to actually live there all the time to get on their radar, do you?"

"I suppose not," Cole agreed. Nashville wasn't really that far, less than a day's drive. Plus, as far as he knew, the other guys had no interest in moving to Nashville. Music was more of a hobby for them, and they were happy playing local gigs.

Cole supposed that it was time to start ring-shopping. This wasn't the first time Chelsea had brought up getting married and he knew that it was the next logical step. Truth be told, it would be the easiest thing for him to do. He'd dated plenty of girls and finally had to accept that he wasn't likely to find what he had with Laura with anyone else. Chelsea was a great girl. They got along well enough and he wouldn't mind having a 'home base', as she had put it. He liked the idea of settling down and wasn't keen on the alternative—starting over with someone. While he might not be head over heels in love with Chelsea, he figured that he probably loved her enough.

CHAPTER 13

The next month was a whirlwind. Laura met with a few possible backup bands and clicked with the one that Ricky had mentioned when they first met. The guys in the band were talented musicians, all a few years older than her, except for the drummer, Jimmy who was the same age. Tom was on bass guitar, and Dylan played the lead guitar. Tom and Jimmy were brothers and looked it, with bright red hair and freckles.

Once they were all comfortable with each other, Ricky lined up their first gigs around town. This was nothing new for the rest of the band but for Laura, it was huge—terrifying and exhilarating at the same time. It felt entirely different from the many writer's nights she'd done because those never felt like they were about her—it was always the song.

During the day, Laura had also started to record at the studio which was more exciting than anything she'd experienced so far. The hours flew by as she sang the same songs over and over again, and she never minded. She was fascinated by the whole process, adding in different effects and background tracks and trying slightly different spins on her delivery.

On the Friday before her first gig, she was in the studio working on one of the newest songs when Harry stopped by to listen for a bit and to wish her luck.

"Ricky tells me tonight is your first official performance. You're probably a little nervous?"

"I am," she admitted.

Harry smiled. "It's normal. Use it to your advantage. Just focus on the music. It only takes one song that breaks out and you're on your way. Wouldn't surprise me if it's the one you were just working on. Are you planning to sing that one tonight?"

"I'm not sure, actually. Dylan was working on the playlist. We've practiced it, though, so we could."

"Tell him I suggested you add it. And pay attention to how the crowd reacts."

"Okay, I'll tell him."

It was a different feeling to be part of a scheduled act and paid performers instead of wannabes waiting for a turn to sing. Laura felt like pinching herself when she wasn't feeling sick with nerves. The Spire was a place that she'd only been to a few times since she moved to town. They were known for having great local bands and up-and-comers to keep an eye on. They charged a cover and Laura and her friends mostly went to the smaller venues and the open mic nights. This was something else entirely.

The energy in the air felt electric. She could hear the hum of the crowd, laughter, and conversations. A quick peek from backstage showed that the room was almost entirely full, and all the tables and seats near the stage were taken. Hundreds of people, waiting to hear music— her music. She swallowed nervously, hoping that she wouldn't disappoint them.

"You'll do fine." Dylan appeared by her side and gave her shoulder a reassuring squeeze.

"Thanks. I'm trying not to think about being nervous."

"Just follow my lead. Find a focal point in the audience and look that way and just feel the music, let it go through you. You know what to do."

"You guys ready? You're on in five." Tony, the bar manager, came back to check on them before disappearing back into the crowd.

"Let's do this." Dylan grabbed her hand and led her to their set up on stage. Laura lifted her guitar over her shoulder and adjusted it, feeling safer behind it. She wouldn't be playing the way that the others would be, just strumming along, so she could focus on her vocals, but she was happy to do that.

The background music faded, and Tony bounded on stage to introduce them to the crowd.

"Everyone, you're in for a treat. This is Laura Scott's official first gig with her new band. She recently signed with Black Duck and is working on a CD. Enjoy!"

When the music started, Laura took a deep breath and

looked around the room to find her focal point. For a moment she felt dizzy as the swarm of people was overwhelming, but she forced the fear down. The familiar melody swept over her, and she began to sing, trying to disappear into the music, but she was still overly aware of the audience. She sensed that her voice was a little wobbly at first but it evened out and when the song ended, there was polite applause.

They were on the last song of their first set when Dylan looked around and said, "A slight change in order. Let's do Breaking Down now and First Love in the second set." Breaking Down was the song Harry had suggested they add. First Love was her very first song, which was still her favorite. It was a softer melody whereas Breaking Down was more of an attention getter.

"Fine by me," she said.

The tempo to the song had a different energy, more upbeat. And as she sang, Laura sensed a shift of interest in the crowd. People chatting less, and leaning forward to listen. It was a fun song to sing, and the lyrics were catchier. It was easier for her to lose herself in the song. When she finished, there was a moment of silence that was electrifying, and then the audience erupted in enthusiastic applause.

Dylan grinned and gave her a thumbs up. "You nailed it!" he said as they walked off-stage for a twenty-minute break between their two sets.

When they came back on, Laura noticed a difference. During most of the first set, the crowd had been listening but not really fully engaged until her last song. She supposed she couldn't blame them. They'd never heard of her before, and she knew she wasn't quite herself for most of the set. But now, they seemed eager to hear more.

They started with another one of her newer songs and finished the set with First Love. Dylan had suggested during the break that she say a few words before it, to thank them all for coming and help them to get to know her a bit. It was one thing to sing, with the band supporting her, but to directly address a crowd this size was daunting. But she recognized a good idea when she heard it.

She took a step forward and smiled at the crowd before speaking. "Thank you all for coming tonight. I really appreciate it. We all do." She then introduced all the members of the band and the audience clapped politely for each of them. "This last song is special to me. It's actually the very first song I wrote, though it's gone through many changes over the years. This is the latest version. I hope you like it."

As she always did with this song, Laura disappeared into the music. It was a part of her, and she still didn't know where this song came from, but it spoke to her and from the reaction it usually got on open mic nights, it connected with others, too. Tonight was no exception. When she finished singing, the crowd was on their feet as one, clapping and hollering. It was the biggest reaction she'd received yet, and it was surprising and so gratifying. She glanced over at Dylan, and he was looking at the crowd. When he turned her way, he had an expression that she couldn't read, but he looked pleased.

"I think they want more," he said.

"Really?" She hadn't even considered the possibility of an encore.

"Yeah. Let's do Magic." Magic was another new song that they'd only done a few times together, but Laura knew it was one of her best.

They launched into the song and Laura was having the time of her life. The song was electric, and the crowd was loving it. The applause when they finished made that clear.

"First round is on me," Dylan said when they left the stage. They were all on a high.

The hours had flown by, and she didn't want the night to end. Tina, Rufus, and Jason were all there. Laura stopped by their table to say hello before joining the rest of the band.

"Is it always like that?" she asked as Dylan pulled out a chair for her to join them at their table where they were all drinking beer. A moment later a waitress came by to get her a drink, and she ordered a glass of wine.

Dylan exchanged amused glances with the others and shook his head. "No, it's not. But when it is, it's really something else. That was special tonight. I knew you were good, but man, that was something."

"It was fun."

Dylan lifted his glass and the others raised theirs. "Here's to many more nights like this one!"

CHAPTER 14

C ole picked up on the many hints that Chelsea not so subtly dropped about the style of wedding ring that she preferred. He presented her with a two-carat cushion-cut diamond surrounded by a ring of tiny diamonds in a platinum setting. He knew he'd done well when she caught her breath then flung her arms around his neck and kissed him senseless.

He happily agreed to let her do whatever she wanted for the wedding. His father had advised him that it would be easier that way since they both knew she was going to want a lavish wedding and Cole didn't want to be bothered with the details. Her family was paying for it, and it didn't matter much to Cole what they did. He planned to just show up when they told him to, wearing the tux they'd picked out and enjoy the day as best he could.

It went pretty much as expected, though the wedding was even bigger than he'd anticipated. The final count for guests exceeded 600 and Cole had no idea who more than half of them were. Chelsea met with his father several times to go over the guest list, adding more names to it each time. Their wedding was a big deal in Charleston. Anyone who was anyone was invited, and just about everyone said yes. Those who sent regrets seemed to really mean it, according to Chelsea. Cole smiled at the absurdity of it.

For Chelsea, though, planning their wedding was almost a second job. It consumed most of her non-working hours. She was determined that it be memorable and no expense was spared. There was going to be an outdoor reception on the grounds of the Plantation, with twinkling lights and tents everywhere. Cole worried about rain, but Chelsea had a backup plan for that too. A nearby hall was rented and on standby, in case the weather drove them inside.

Otherwise, it would be a beautiful evening with an in-demand band and a portable wood floor for dancing. No detail had been overlooked. And even though she'd planned the wedding thoroughly, Chelsea still used a wedding planner to make sure that all her demands were carried out and so Chelsea would be able to focus on enjoying and networking at her wedding.

Cole was well aware that their wedding was an opportunity for Chelsea to network with many of the most important people in the city who were otherwise inaccessible, but through his father's connections, would be at the wedding. The same went for his father. It was an opportunity for him to hold court and Cole knew his father would be in his glory, working the crowd to build support and cement existing relationships so that he could count on them for future elections. There was no doubt that there would be future elections. Cole was certain that his father's ambitions went beyond being governor.

Everything went off perfectly. Chelsea was exquisite in a white dress that fit her slim figure snugly before flowing behind her. The weather cooperated and couldn't have been better. Even the bugs stayed away, thanks to heavy spraying the day before.

They had moved into the Plantation house unofficially the week before, having all of their furniture delivered. The night of the wedding would be the first time they actually slept there, though, and only for one night before they left for their honeymoon, a Western Caribbean cruise.

"You look so serious," Chelsea teased him near the end of the evening when she appeared by his side. The crowd was starting to thin out, and people were finally going home. Cole stood alone by one of the many bars and was sipping a fresh Jack and Coke as he gazed at the crowd.

"I'm just tired. I think everyone had a good time," he said.

"Of course they did. I made sure of it," Chelsea said with a laugh.

He smiled at her. "You did a great job. Everyone has raved about everything—the cake, the band, the food."

The food had been amazing. There were stations for just about anything a guest could desire, from pasta to various meats and shellfish. Even Maine lobster tails had been flown in. Not to mention endless passed appetizers. Neither one of them had eaten much, though. They had been busy making the rounds and talking to people.

"It has been an amazing night," she agreed. She leaned in and spoke softly. "Your father came through again. He introduced me to Bernie Shaeffer, and he invited me to meet with him when we get back from our honeymoon. There may be a job opening up at his firm that I could be good for."

Cole smiled. His new wife was far more driven than he was, but he was happy for her.

"That's great. I'm sure he will love you."

Chelsea laughed "Of course he will. But not as much as you do, right?" She gave him a playful kiss and Cole kissed her back distractedly. He tried to focus on how beautiful his new wife looked and to ignore the memories of Laura that had been haunting him all day. He kept reminding himself that what they'd had was rare and he wasn't likely to find it again in this lifetime. And that what he had with Chelsea was pretty darn good, too. They could be happy together and build a future. He was certain of it.

CHAPTER 15

EIGHT MONTHS LATER...

Chelsea rushed around the kitchen, making coffee and splashing milk into a microwaved bowl of oatmeal while Cole calmly sipped his coffee and watched her. Chelsea was always in a hurry, even on a Friday which was a more laid back day than most. She joined him at the kitchen table and ate quickly while he gazed at the morning paper.

"So what will you be up to this weekend while I'm gone?" he asked as she took her last bite. He'd reminded her earlier in the week that he was going to Nashville for the weekend, but she'd barely acknowledged it. It seemed to have slipped her mind completely, or maybe it just never registered as being important.

"This weekend?" She hesitated for a moment and then laughed as she dropped her spoon into her empty bowl.

"No plans, really. Maybe I'll go out with people for an after work drink."

"Oh? With your co-workers?" Cole hadn't met any of them but knew she occasionally went out for drinks with some of them after work.

She nodded. "Maybe. Depends how I feel. I'm sure you'll have more fun than I will." She dropped her empty dish and coffee mug in the sink and gave him a quick peck on the lips to say goodbye. "I have to run. See you on Sunday." And then she was gone. Her car pulled out of the driveway a moment later. He felt a little blue as he took his last sip of coffee.

Chelsea was so busy lately, and seemed distant and preoccupied all the time. He knew that she was under a lot of stress with her job, but he also knew that she loved it. Her job was all-consuming. By the time she got home at night she was exhausted. Lately, he'd been feeling like they were more roommates than anything else. The romance in their relationship had definitely cooled. He asked her about it once. She'd just laughed it off and said they were a normal married couple. It didn't feel normal to Cole, though. Not for the first time, he wondered how it would have been if he and Laura had never been in that accident. If they'd gotten married, had their baby and lived their lives.

He rinsed out his coffee mug and Chelsea's dishes, too, and put everything in the dishwasher. Fifteen minutes later, he was on the road toward Nashville. He had a room booked for the night at an inexpensive hotel. He was looking forward to relaxing once he got there and checking out some local spots that often featured new artists. It wouldn't be a late night, though.

He needed to get a good night's sleep as tomorrow was going to be a long day. He'd been invited by one of the junior producers of the hit show New Voices to come in for an audition. They'd seen a few of his YouTube clips. Cole was over the moon excited when he got the call, but the producer was quick to explain that it was far from a sure thing. He'd be one of many new artists that were invited to audition.

He mentioned it to Chelsea when he got the call but she didn't really share his excitement. Her nose had wrinkled as if she'd smelled something unpleasant.

"You're going to audition for a reality TV show? Are you sure that's a good idea? Did you tell Dalton?"

As if he needed to ask his father's permission. He had no intention of telling him unless he was chosen for the show and he'd cross that bridge if it happened. The guys in his band had seemed thrilled for him, and maybe just a little envious. They weren't playing as many gigs as he'd hoped. They all had other jobs that were their focus now and Cole was still busy with his last year of law school. Just getting the call felt like a big step to him. A validation that someone out there recognized that he had talent. So, it was a disappointment that his wife didn't get how important it was. Instead, she was concerned with appearances, as usual.

Cole sighed as he reached the exit for I 26W and turned onto the highway. He zoned out as he drove, listening to the current country hits. Hours later, as he reached the outskirts of Nashville, the radio announcer introduced a new song and artist. He didn't catch her name as he wasn't paying close enough attention, but something about her sound seemed familiar. She was good, really good, and there was a haunting rasp to her voice as she sang about her first love. It was a bittersweet song and it gave him chills. He didn't know who she was, but he had a sense the song would be a hit. He knew how difficult it was to get airtime with a major station as a new artist, so they likely recognized it, too. As the song ended, he waited to hear her name mentioned again, and when it came, he nearly drove off the road.

COLE CHECKED into his hotel in a daze. He picked up a newspaper in the lobby that had listings of which bands were playing at all the local clubs and brought it up to his room. His original plan had been to just check out a few of his favorite places. But now, he was looking for one artist in particular. Laura.

He still couldn't believe it was his Laura on the radio. It didn't make any sense. She'd never shown any interest in music before, other than to support him. He'd never heard her sing before which is why he didn't recognize her at first. He thought back and couldn't remember her so much as even humming along to a song.

He found what he was looking for on the second page of the listings. Laura Scott was going to be singing at one of the bigger clubs. His stomach grumbled, reminding him that he hadn't eaten all day and it was suppertime. He'd take a quick shower, grab a burger somewhere and then make his way over to the bar. He was curious to hear what else she had for songs and to see her, maybe catch up. He wondered if she was married now. If she ever thought of him.

Since his wedding day, Cole hadn't thought of Laura at all, until recently. She'd crossed his mind a few times lately as Chelsea was spending more time at the office, and she'd been distant and short with him. She always apologized and blamed it on lack of sleep and long hours. They didn't spend as much time together as they used to. And so, more than once Laura had crossed his mind.

He still missed the easy and sweet friendship that he'd shared with Laura. He'd loved her, but she was also his best friend. But, he reminded himself that it was her choice to go. To take his father's money and leave town. It still didn't seem like the Laura he knew. But it was hard to refute what he knew to be true. Still, it would be nice to see her.

THERE WAS a good crowd at the bar when he arrived. He settled into an empty seat that had a good view of the stage and ordered a beer. A few minutes later the opening band came on, and they were pretty good. The crowd gave them an enthusiastic round of applause when they finished their set. Cole ordered a second beer during the brief break between acts. When the lights flashed to indicate the band was about to come on, he noticed a shift in the room's energy. There was a sense of anticipation.

Laura and her band were introduced and took their places on the stage. Cole watched, mesmerized. She looked as good as he remembered, yet she seemed a stranger as she confidently welcomed the crowd and introduced the guys in the band. They launched into a song Laura said was called Magic. It was the perfect name. Whoever wrote her songs was gifted. The melody was catchy, and the lyrics were haunting. And Laura's voice, with its soft, raspy quality, was addicting.

The next hour flew as they sang song after song, all of them wonderful in their own way. Cole felt goosebumps several times when she started a new song, and he recognized how good it was. How good she was. He'd never been one to predict the future, but he knew in his bones that Laura was going to go far. It wouldn't be long before Laura Scott was a household name. He was thrilled for her and perplexed at the same time. He was also full of questions. How did this happen? How long had she been singing? Why had she never told him that she shared the same dream?

Laura closed the night with the song he'd heard on the radio. Listening to it again, he realized with a shock that Laura was singing about him and their love. Her voice broke with emotion as she sang the final note and Cole had to fight the urge to run to her and pull her into his arms. Because of course, he couldn't do that. Shouldn't even be thinking that way. He felt guilty as he thought of Chelsea, his wife. He had to talk to Laura, though, to ask his questions.

When she finished singing, the band all bowed. The guy on guitar put his arm around Laura's shoulders, and she smiled up at him. They kissed briefly and it was clear to Cole that they were together. He felt himself frowning as he saw it and when he noticed that neither of them was wearing a wedding ring, he felt a sense of relief. Which was ridiculous, of course. He knew that. He felt like a confused teenager again, being so close to Laura and so full of questions.

Fifteen minutes later, Laura and the guitar player walked toward the bar. When they were about a foot away from him, Laura caught his eye and smiled as Dylan got the bartender's attention.

"Hi, Laura," Cole said. "You guys were great."

"Thank you. I'm glad you enjoyed the show," she said politely. It was as if she was talking to a stranger.

"It's nice to see you. I didn't realize you'd gotten into singing."

A look of confusion crossed Laura's face, and Cole realized that she was trying to place him. Finally, she spoke.

"I'm so sorry, have we met?"

"We went to school together, in Charleston. I'm Cole, Cole Dalton."

Laura looked even more confused. "I think you may have me confused with someone else. I never went to school in Charleston. I'm from Montana."

Cole almost dropped the beer that he was holding.

"Is this guy bothering you?" Dylan said as he handed Laura a beer.

"Oh, no. Not at all." Laura sounded flustered.

"Good. It looks like the guys found a table, let's head over." He walked off, expecting Laura to follow.

"Have a good night, Cole," she said as she turned to follow Dylan.

Cole watched her walk off before asking the bartender for a shot of whiskey and his tab. He rarely drank the hard stuff, but it seemed appropriate. He also realized that he'd be paying his father a visit on the way home tomorrow. Dalton Dawson had some explaining to do.

Laura slid into the chair that Dylan pulled out for her when they reached the roundtable where the rest of the band was sitting. She took a sip of her beer and found herself yawning a moment later. The night had caught up with her. It had gone well, though. She glanced over at the bar where the handsome blonde guy had been sitting, Cole something. He was gone now, his seat empty.

Funny how he seemed so sure that he knew her. He was a good-looking guy, and while there was something vaguely familiar about him, she was sure that she'd never met him before. She'd also been surprised by the wave of attraction that had hit her when he turned her way and spoke. If they had met before, she wouldn't have forgotten that.

"That's probably going to start happening to you more often, you know." Dylan looked at her protectively.

"People thinking they know me?" She smiled. "I think he just got me mixed up with someone else."

"Maybe. But people are going to want to meet you, get close to you. You have to be on guard more. That's all I'm saying." He reached over and took one of her hands, squeezing it reassuringly. They'd been together for three months now. It had just sort of happened. The band spent so much time together, and Dylan was good company. Besides, she had to admit, his interest was flattering. He was a good-looking guy, though a little more possessive than she was used to.

He was ten years older than her, too, and though it wasn't a big difference, sometimes she felt the gap in their ages. Dylan could be bossy, though whenever she complained about it, he explained that he was just looking out for her. Lately, she sensed that he wanted to get more serious and she found herself pulling back a little. She wasn't ready for that, with anyone. She had too much going on in her life and singing had to be her number one focus.

The past two weeks, since her CD officially released, had been a whirlwind. They were actually playing her music on the radio now, which was surreal. Dylan was sure that she was going to make the top ten on the Billboard chart. But Laura didn't dare dream that big. Top 100 would be mind-blowing. They'd know in a few days. Billboard updated the lists every Tuesday.

"So, Laura, I have a question for you." Dylan's voice snapped Laura's attention back. She looked his way and then froze. All the other guys in the band were leaning forward and smiling expectantly. Dylan was on his knees, in front of her, holding a small black velvet box. Her throat and chest suddenly felt tight. He couldn't be doing what it looked like he was doing, in front of everyone?

Dylan grinned as he opened the box and Laura gasped. Inside sat a gorgeous emerald-cut diamond, surrounded by a delicate row of tiny diamonds. It was a beautiful ring—if someone wanted to get engaged.

"So, what do you think? Will you do me the honor of saying yes? I love you, Laura Scott. I want to spend the rest of my life with you."

Laura swallowed nervously. There was a long silence, and she knew she had to speak, to say something before it became uncomfortable. She forced herself to smile.

"I love you, too. Of course I'll marry you." What else was she supposed to say? She couldn't very well say no in front of all his friends. But they were going to talk later.

CHAPTER 16

Cole slept horribly. It was a combination of a saggy bed, more alcohol than he usually drank in an evening and seeing Laura. He'd imagined seeing her again many times, but never like this. He'd thought she'd be glad to see him, and that they'd at least be able to reminisce and catch up. Impossible to do, though, when she didn't even remember him. How could that be? She must have been more badly hurt than his father had told him. And Cole had a sneaking suspicion that there was more to the story. Because why wouldn't his father have told him that she had memory loss? He was going to find out.

He had to be at the Nashville studios where the show was filmed by eight a.m. The producer he'd spoken to had told him to plan on being there for four or five hours at least. They were holding auditions all week and would keep going until each of the four judges filled up their team of twelve artists. Cole had long been a fan of the show. He liked the way the chosen artists received individual coaching, and the camaraderie among the judges was fun to watch.

Cole wondered if Laura had ever tried out for a show like this. He was still in shock and awe at what she'd done for herself so far. He wondered if he would ever have the chance to talk to her and hear her story. After what she'd said at the bar, somehow he doubted it. He was a stranger to her now.

When Cole arrived at the studio, it was already bustling. He was directed to one of the large waiting areas full of other hopefuls like himself. He glanced around the room. Everyone looked as excited and as nervous as he felt. And he knew they were likely all good, too, or they wouldn't be there. He took a deep breath and tried not to let his nerves get the best of him. He didn't usually have issues with stage fright. But he wasn't feeling his usual confident self. When he got on stage at home, he knew he was good. Here, he was just one of many. Who knew what the judges were looking for?

One by one, people were called to audition. Once they left the room, they never came back, so there was no way of knowing how well anyone had done. Finally, when the room was almost empty except for Cole and one other person, his name was called. Cole followed Amelia, the young aide who led him to the stage where the judges were waiting. The lights were strong, so that he couldn't see any of them particularly well. No one spoke, and Cole was told earlier that he'd go right into singing and the judges would talk to him when he finished.

The familiar music started. Cole began to sing, but it didn't feel right. He felt off, not one with the music like he usually was. He tried to shake off his nerves and focus, and by the last quarter of the song, he settled in and knew he was in the zone. But would it be too late?

There was a long moment of silence and then Gary Jones, the grouchy head judge asked, "Do you have another song you could sing? We need to hear a little more before we decide."

"Sure. I'm happy to." And he was. The music for his backup song came on, and this time Cole was in the zone from the beginning. He gave it his all, and he knew when he finished that he'd nailed it. He'd shown them what he wanted them to see.

Gary was smiling. "I think the nerves got a hold of you in your first song. We got a glimpse of what you could do toward the end. I'm glad you sang again for us. I'd love to have you on my team. But I think the others would, too, so you get to choose who you want for your coach."

All four judges had raised their hands to indicate that they wanted Cole on their team. Each one had nice things to say, and Cole was torn on who to go with. He closed his eyes for a moment and didn't think, he just felt and then went with his gut instinct.

"Thank you all so much. Gary, I'd be honored to be on your team."

"Fantastic. Be back here in one month. That's when we'll start shooting. Congratulations!"

Cole hit the road as soon as he left the studio and pulled into the driveway of his father's Charleston house around eight thirty that night. He didn't bother to call first. He saw his father's car and knew that he was home. He knocked when he reached the door but didn't bother to wait for a response. He let himself in and looked around. He could see there was a glow from the television in the den.

He walked into the room, and his father looked up in surprise. He turned off the television and raised his eyebrows.

"Is something wrong?"

Cole crossed the room and sat in an armchair opposite his father. "I just got back from Nashville."

"Hm. That's nice, I suppose. Did you have a good time?"

"I had a very interesting time. It was an eventful trip. You know that show New Voices?"

"The singing one?"

"That's it. I auditioned this morning and was selected to be on the show."

"You're going to be on a reality show? And that is a good thing?" His father looked dismayed by the thought of it.

"It could be a very good thing. It might lead to something. A recording deal."

His father stared out the window for a moment. But it was dark outside, and there was nothing to see. Finally, he spoke, "I'd hoped you were over that nonsense. You're about to graduate from law school, start your career."

"I've always been clear with you that this is my first choice, Dad. You know that."

His father said nothing. After a long moment of silence, Cole changed the subject to discuss what was really on his mind.

"I saw Laura Scott in Nashville."

His father's eyes narrowed, and Cole noticed a flicker of a muscle along his jaw.

"Laura Scott?"

"Yes. Though it was the strangest thing. She didn't seem to remember me."

Cole wasn't sure, but for a fleeting second, he thought he saw a hint of a smile flash across his father's face. But then it was gone. He must have imagined it. His father looked deep in thought again but said nothing.

"Dad, why wouldn't Laura remember me? What happened to her in the accident? Is there something you didn't tell me?"

His father sighed and looked uncomfortable, a bit guilty even.

"Laura may have had some memory issues," he said finally.

"What kind of memory issues?"

"The doctor said it was the worst case of amnesia he'd ever seen."

"Amnesia? But you said Laura chose to go to Montana and took your money."

"She did. Sort of." He looked decidedly uncomfortable now as Cole felt his anger build. The urge to hit something was strong, and he wasn't a violent person. He clenched his fist and glared his father, urging him silently to continue.

"The doctor said she might get her memory back if she was around familiar places and people."

When Cole realized what that meant, he looked at his father in horror.

"What did you do?"

"I did what I thought was best for you. And for her. She went to live with your Aunt Helen, and I paid for her college expenses."

"Is she aware of that?" Cole couldn't remember ever being so furious.

"No, I don't suppose she was. She and your Aunt Helen got along well, I heard."

Cole felt betrayed by both his father and his aunt. "Why would Aunt Helen agree to do that?" Cole had always liked his aunt. After thinking about it for a moment, he realized why.

"You paid for Harold's care, didn't you?"

His father nodded. "The facility he went to was quite expensive. Helen didn't have that kind of money. I was happy to help."

"I bet you were." Cole stood. "I can't believe you did that to her, and to Laura and me. She would have remembered me. She should have had the chance to try!"

His father shifted in his seat and looked away. "I'm sorry, Cole. I did what I thought was best for everyone. I hope that someday, you'll understand that."

"I'm not sure that I'll ever be able to forgive you. You went way too far."

"It was a long time ago, Cole. You're happily married now, and Laura seems to be doing well enough." He stood, too, and smiled the charming smile that usually got him what he wanted. "Will we see you and Chelsea as usual for dinner after church tomorrow?" Every Sunday, Chelsea and Cole met his father and Claire at the club after church.

Cole narrowed his eyes. "How do you know how Laura is doing?"

"Well, I'm assuming she is doing well. They've been playing that song of hers non-stop on the radio this past week."

"No, Chelsea and I will not be joining you at the club tomorrow or anytime in the near future. I mean it, Dad. You really crossed the line."

"I meant well. You know that. When you calm down, you'll realize that."

Cole shook his head in disgust. "I'm going home now."

DYLAN WANTED to celebrate after Laura accepted his proposal and he had a bottle of champagne ready on ice. They all drank it and he ordered another. Somehow word got out quickly, and it seemed as though almost the entire crowd at the bar came by to congratulate them. Out of the corner of her eye, Laura noticed a few pictures being taken and sighed. She knew the news of her engagement would be in the paper tomorrow and was probably already all over Facebook and Instagram. She shuddered at the thought of it. She still didn't have a Facebook account and had no desire for one, but the studio's marketing department handled social media for her, and they set up a page and a Twitter feed. She didn't care what they did as long as she didn't have to try to figure out social media.

Laura didn't have the heart to burst Dylan's bubble when they got home later that night. Instead, she decided to have the conversation over coffee the next morning and was already dreading it.

THE COFFEE WAS DELICIOUS, but Dylan didn't seem to be enjoying it. He pouted while Laura tried to explain that it seemed a bit too soon to be engaged.

"Are you saying you don't want to marry me?"

Laura sighed. "I'm saying that it's just so fast. I might want to at some point, but we've only been dating a few months. I honestly hadn't even considered it yet."

"But you said you love me."

"I did say that," Laura agreed. She didn't add that she'd felt pressured into saying it and that it was unfair to do that publicly.

"So, what's the problem then? We don't have to set a date yet. We can have a long engagement if you like. That's fine with me." Dylan's eyes were big and pleading. Laura felt a headache beginning to brew. She pressed her hands on her forehead and Dylan looked concerned.

"What's wrong? Are you sick? Do you want an aspirin?"

She shook her head. "I'll be fine. I'm just tired. Coffee will help. I suppose we could do a long engagement." It seemed easier to just agree for the time being.

Dylan grinned and wrapped his arms around her.

"You're perfect. We're going to have the best life together."

Laura smiled and nodded as she topped off her coffee. She needed to keep her focus on the music. Dylan and their relationship needed to take a back-burner, at least for now.

CHAPTER 17

Cole was still fuming when he got home. Usually the swaying willows that lined the driveway of the Plantation house calmed and soothed him. Tonight, they didn't even register as he grabbed his overnight bag out of the back seat and walked into the house. Chelsea was sprawled out on the family room sofa, painting her toenails. She looked up when he walked in.

"How was your trip?"

Cole set his bag down and joined her on the sofa. "It was good. Long, but worthwhile. I made it to the show."

She sat up and faced him. "You did? Well, that's great news, right?"

Cole smiled and felt himself finally start to relax. "Yeah, it's really good news."

Chelsea looked concerned. "Is something else wrong? You don't seem as excited as I would have expected."

Cole sighed. "It's my father. I found out that he lied to

me about Laura and what was really going on after the accident."

"What do you mean?"

"She didn't choose to end our relationship and to move across the country. She completely lost her memory. He sent her far away from anything familiar that would help her to remember."

Chelsea didn't react the way that he would have expected. She was quiet for a moment and then said, "Well, I'm sure he had a good reason. He must have thought he was doing what was best for you." She almost sounded as if it was a perfectly reasonable thing to do.

He shook his head in disgust. "How can you say that? Laura and I were in love. We were going to get married."

"Well, maybe if it was that important to her, she would have remembered. Have you ever thought of that?" Chelsea's tone was a little impatient.

Cole knew she didn't like when he mentioned Laura but still, the remark stung. Because of course the thought had crossed his mind. How could Laura have forgotten about him, about their love? It was hard to fathom, but he didn't blame her for it. He knew that sometimes these things happened and no one really knew why.

He supposed he shouldn't be too surprised that Chelsea wasn't overly sympathetic. She idolized his father and was sure he had a good reason for what he did. But Chelsea didn't know his father the way Cole did. Dalton Dawson was ruthless even toward his son if he was in his way, and Cole's love for Laura was a problem that needed to be dealt with. Still, he'd never imagined his father would go this far.

Cole leaned back on the sofa and put his feet up on the coffee table knocking something small off the edge. He reached to pick it up and raised his eyes at Chelsea when he saw what it was, a plastic stick with one pink line.

"Are you..."

"Pregnant?" Chelsea laughed. "No! Thank goodness. I had a scare though, I really thought I was at first. I think we should wait another year or two until I'm more established at work." She bit her lower lip, something she did when she was trying to think something through. "I don't know what I would have done if it was positive."

Cole felt like his emotions were on a see-saw. "What are you saying? You would have wanted to get rid of our baby?" His hands clenched together again and he stared at her, shocked at what he'd just heard.

"Well, no. I wouldn't necessarily want to. But it's not really a baby yet, is it? It's so early, and people do it all the time. I thought we should maybe at least consider it. But, the good news is, we don't have to worry about it!"

Cole shook his head. "I don't know how you could even think like that. I would have been excited about our baby."

Chelsea nodded. "Forget I even mentioned it then." She smiled but Cole just shook his head. He could understand her being nervous as it was a big responsibility to have a child. But, to seriously consider getting rid of it if she was?

He felt a wave of sadness as he remembered how excited both he and Laura had been when she found out she was pregnant. They were both scared, but there was never a moment of doubt with either of them that they wanted to have their baby. He sighed, thinking about Laura. About what they'd shared, and now she didn't even remember him. It was like he never existed.

IT WAS AMAZING how quickly things changed for Laura. The first Tuesday after her single released it hit #5 on the Billboard country chart. The week after that it went to #2 behind a new Kenny Chesney tune, and it stuck there for five weeks. Suddenly, everyone wanted to know all about her. Invitations began pouring in. People magazine even called and wanted to include her along with four other new country artists for a special feature on 'people to watch'.

Laura, Dylan, Tina, and Rufus went out to dinner on a rare Saturday night that Laura didn't have a booking somewhere. They went to dinner at a local spot they all liked. Two minutes after they'd sat down, a young woman about their age came over and said she was with one of the local papers and would Laura mind if she snapped a picture. She took her picture and left. Tina commented the minute she was away from the table.

"Well, aren't you the big star now," she teased.

"Hardly. It is weird, though, people recognizing me and wanting pictures."

"I bet that is hard to get used to," Tina said. Laura smiled, thinking that Tina would be so much better suited to all the attention. Laura understood that it went with the job, but it was the hardest part for her. She was naturally shy and preferred not to be the center of attention. But, it was unavoidable. The last thing she wanted to do was to complain about it.

"I think it's a good problem to have. I feel very lucky," Laura said.

"She really is going to be a big star," Dylan said.

Laura cringed. She'd never think of herself that way, no matter how well things went for her. "I'm really not. Let's change the subject," she insisted. Dylan smiled and pulled her against him.

"Let's talk about that ring. Dylan, you did well," Tina said as she lifted Laura's hand to take a closer look. It really was a pretty ring, Laura had to admit. Everyone at the studio was in favor of the engagement. Harry thought people would think it was romantic and so far, he was right. Laura was surprised that anyone even cared, but she was learning that country music fans were interested in everything about her.

"He did do well. It's beautiful," Laura agreed, and Dylan looked happy to hear it. "What about you? What's new in your world?" Tina had moved in with Rufus a month ago. Laura missed her, but she was so busy that she hadn't seen Tina much in the weeks before she moved.

"Well, I have some news, too. You know how we weren't in any rush to get married?"

Laura nodded.

"Well, we're getting married in two weeks. I hope you'll still stand up with me? We're just going to do it at town hall."

"What? Why? Of course." Laura wondered why the sudden change in plans.

Tina laughed. "Well, I have more news. I'd been feeling really crappy for over a month and finally went to the doctor. I thought I had a bug. It turns out I'm pregnant!"

A wave of happy emotion swept of Laura, taking her by surprise. "That's wonderful news. Are you excited?"

Tina nodded. "Yes. We both are. It's happening sooner than we expected, but we're kind of thrilled, to be honest."

Laura gave her a big hug. "You'll be a wonderful mother."

Dylan watched their exchange with interest. He offered his congratulations to both Tina and Rufus and a little while later asked Laura, "You're not in any rush to have kids, are you?"

"No, why?"

"Just wondering. We never really talked about it. I think it would be good to wait, at least five years or so. Don't you?"

"I really haven't given it a thought."

COLE DIDN'T SEE or talk to his father again until his law school graduation almost a month later. He grudgingly agreed to go to lunch at the club after the ceremony with his father, Claire and her boys. He was surprised to find that his Aunt Helen had flown in for the occasion as well. He had mixed feelings about seeing her. They'd always been close, but he was still unhappy about her involvement in his father's deception with Laura. Yet, at the same time, he understood why she did it. She looked hesitant when she saw him and Cole immediately knew that his father had let her know about their conversation.

"I'm glad you came," he said simply as they hugged each other hello.

"I'm so proud of you, and I'm so very sorry." Her voice broke as she spoke and her eyes welled up.

Cole sighed. "I understand why you did it. He's the one I'm upset with."

Aunt Helen nodded and looked somewhat relieved.

Chelsea stood nearby, looking confused. Cole hadn't told her anything about the conversation with his father or about Laura. There was no point to it.

"It's been a long time since I've seen her," he explained as they drove to the club together. "Are you feeling any better?" Chelsea had a horrible hangover. She'd gone out the night before with the girls and Cole had no idea what time she'd come home.

She nodded. "I took a few Advils, and they finally kicked in. I'm ready for a good meal now."

The club was packed. Sunday afternoons were always busy, but there were other graduations happening and the dining room was fully booked. They had a reservation, though, and were seated right away. As they made their way to the table, his father was stopped several times. Everyone seemed to know him. It had always been like that, but even more so now that he was the Governor.

They had a surprisingly amicable meal. The food was good, and his father was more charming than usual, telling funny stories and complimenting the women on how beautiful they looked. He always had been charismatic and larger than life. Cole's father thrived on being the center of attention. Being a politician suited him. Cole was still furious with him, though. He didn't know if he'd ever be able to forgive him.

"Chelsea, you're positively glowing today. That color suits you."

Chelsea beamed at Cole's father. She sought his approval and had always been impressed by his success. He'd also helped her by introducing her to several of his more important friends, and the networking had paid off, first for an internship while in school and then for her current position in public relations. Chelsea hung on every word as his father talked about the various business people and politicians he'd been interacting with that week.

It bored Cole, though. His thoughts began to drift, thinking ahead to his upcoming trip to Nashville. He was excited to be part of the show and hoped that he'd at least stick around for a few weeks. He didn't have any expectations of winning, but he knew that the longer he was able to last, the more connections he'd make. And that was the kind of networking he was happy to engage in.

He loved meeting other people in the music industry,

and talking songs and the business. He also couldn't help thinking about Laura and wondered if he might run into her again. He didn't think it was likely, though, unless he made an effort like he did last time, to find out where she was playing. But, he wasn't sure that was a good idea. In fact, he was pretty sure that it wasn't. Especially now that he had a baby on the way. He needed to keep his priorities straight.

"So, Cole..." At the sound of his name, Cole brought his attention back to his father's words.

"Now that you've graduated, you know there's an open position for you at the firm. You could start as soon as next Monday, if you like." His father sounded both confident and hopeful. Cole just shook his head. His father hadn't listened to him at all. He didn't want to make a scene by reminding him that they weren't really speaking so it was unlikely that he'd want to work for him anytime soon.

"I'm not sure what I'm going to do. I'm not going to be starting anywhere for a while, though. I'm off to Nashville next week and depending on how things go, I might be there for a few weeks or a few months. The longer the better."

His father pursed his lips as if he'd taken a taste of something unexpectedly sour. "Right. I forgot about that show thing. We can discuss when you come back."

"Of course Cole will come work with you then," Chelsea said and shot Cole a look that said "what is wrong with you?!'

Cole squeezed her hand to reassure her. He didn't

want to upset her unnecessarily, especially since she'd been feeling so awful lately.

"I'll get in touch as soon as I get back and we can talk about it then." He had no intention of joining his father's firm, but Chelsea didn't need to know that yet.

CHAPTER 18

Laura spent all day Sunday doing what she loved most, writing songs. She sat in the middle of her living room on a thick, shaggy throw rug, surrounded by notebooks and sheets of paper with scribbles everywhere. She'd lost track of the time completely and jumped when there was a loud knock at the door. It couldn't be Dylan already? She glanced at the clock on the wall and was surprised to see that it was nearly six.

It was Dylan, holding a large pizza box. The smell of tomato and cheese assaulted her senses, making her stomach rumble. She hadn't stopped for lunch. Dylan handed her the box.

"You have that look about you. Have you had anything to eat today?" Dylan opened a bottle of wine while Laura set the pizza on the kitchen table and went to get napkins and plates.

"I had breakfast."

"That's what I figured. Productive day, though?" He poured two glasses of wine and handed one to her.

"It was a great day. First time in ages that I didn't have to go anywhere. It was nice."

They ate and then topped off their wine glasses, brought them into the living room and settled comfortably on the sofa. Dylan seemed to be in a relaxed, mellow mood, and Laura was grateful for it. He'd been somewhat moody lately, and Laura begged off ongoing out twice recently because she just didn't want to deal with it. Staying home alone was more appealing. She sensed that he could tell she was pulling back though because he'd been on his best behavior all week.

Dylan took a sip of wine and then casually said, "So, my lease is up in two months. I need to decide if I want to renew or not."

"Oh?" Laura had a sinking feeling about what was coming next.

"It seems silly for me to renew that lease if we're going to be getting married. Maybe I should just move in here with you?"

A wave of panic came over her.

"Now?"

He laughed. "No, not now. But soon, when my lease is up. I need to let him know if I'm not going to renew."

"Oh, I see."

"So, that's it, then? I'll tell him tomorrow?"

"Do you have to let him know now?" Laura wasn't ready to say yes to Dylan moving in, but she wasn't ready to end their engagement just yet, either. She did like

Dylan. Maybe she even loved him. But it all like felt too much, too fast.

"I have to give him a month's notice. So, a month from now."

"Let's talk about it in a few weeks then. I'm sure it will be fine. It's just that everything is moving so fast lately."

Dylan brushed a wayward strand of hair off her face and kissed her gently.

"Everything is changing for you. But it's all good," he said confidently.

Cole loaded his suitcase in his truck Monday morning and had a second cup of coffee at the kitchen table while he waited for Chelsea to finish getting ready for work. He figured they'd leave together and say their goodbyes. He had no idea how long he'd be gone for. He heard the faint sound of a cell phone ringing, Chelsea's voice answering and a moment later, laughing. Her voice was soft so he couldn't hear what she was saying, just the occasional laugh. He wondered who would be calling so early in the morning and what could possibly be so funny. When she came into the kitchen a few minutes later, he asked her.

"Who was that on the phone?"

She seemed surprised by the question. "Oh, no one. Just someone from the office."

Of course, it was someone from the office. That made sense.

"Busy week?" he asked.

She brightened at the question. Chelsea loved to talk about work. "Yes! We have so much going on. We have some exciting new projects."

"That's great. So, do you think you might be able to make it to Nashville at all? I won't have much of a cheering section." Having someone there to help calm his nerves would be awesome.

Chelsea bit her lip. "I don't think so. I'm sorry. I can't take time off right now, it's much too busy. But you'll do great! I know you will." She wrapped her arms around him and gave him an enthusiastic kiss that was over as soon as it started.

"Good luck, Cole. Text me when you get there, so I know you made it." She walked out ahead of him, climbed into her car and a moment later, she was gone.

THE NEXT MORNING at eight a.m., Cole was in Nashville at the studio along with forty-seven other contestants. Everyone was friendly and most seemed as nervous as he was. There were people from all over the country, ranging in age from fifteen to fifty. And as he quickly learned, everyone was good. Some were so good that it was intimidating. He tried not to let it throw him off-balance, though. He knew that all he could control was his own performance. He'd just go out there and do his best and see what happened. He smiled as he thought of something Laura used to say, "If it's meant to be, it will be."

And for week one, it was meant to be. Cole made it

through the first round, along with twenty-three others. The size of the group had been cut in half. There would be another cut this next week and the week after that, and then the final twelve contestants would move on to the live shows. They'd receive a lot more attention then, and there would be guest coaches coming in each week to give extra guidance to the contestants. Cole hoped that he'd make it to that point. He wanted to go as long as possible but tried to keep his focus on surviving one week at a time.

He really liked working with Gary Jones, his coach. Gary still toured and had an amazing voice. Even though he sometimes came across a bit grouchy, he was passionate about music, and he'd been nothing but encouraging to Cole.

"You're really good, you know. You have a deep, pure voice. There's only one problem." Gary put his hands on his hips and looked Cole in the eye. "You lack conviction. You don't believe that you deserve to be here. You need to get over that and go own that stage. Because you do deserve to be here."

Cole swallowed. He was embarrassed that it was so obvious how he felt. He did feel like he wasn't as good as some of the others and it intimidated him.

"I'm serious. You're as good as anyone here, and you have as much of a chance as they do." He paused and then added, "You could win this thing if you just let go and dig deep. I know you can do it."

"You do?" Cole normally was confident, but this was just so important. There was so much at stake that uncertainty had taken hold and his confidence was shaken.

"Believe, and you can achieve. Sounds hokey, I know. But it's true. If you don't believe in yourself, no one else will. Now, let's hear it again, from the top."

Cole grinned and relaxed. And then he sang like he'd never sung before. When he finished, there was a moment of silence and then the sound of one person clapping. Gary walked over to him, pulled him in for a hug and slapped his back.

"Now, *that* is what I'm talking about."

THE NEXT DAY, for the actual competition, Cole channeled the confidence he'd managed the day before when it was just him and Gary. It felt good, and he was relieved that his performance the day before wasn't a fluke. He did even better and all four judges gave him a standing ovation. They'd only done that for one other contestant so far. He breathed a sigh of relief. He hoped it would be enough to get him through to the next round. And it was. Now, he'd be going on to the live shows.

CHAPTER 19

L aura smiled as she checked her reflection in her bedroom mirror. The dress that the studio had sent fit perfectly and the soft, caramel shade brought out the gold highlights in her hair. She wore it loosely curled. It fell halfway down her back, the longest she'd had it in years.

"You really think it's a good idea to wear that?" Dylan scowled as he appraised her appearance.

Laura's smile faded as she turned to check the back of the dress. Maybe she'd missed something. But no, it looked good to her.

"What's wrong with it?" she asked.

"It's too short, don't you think?" He raised his eyebrows as his gaze hit where her dress stopped, just above her knees. Laura's flash of uncertainty was quickly replaced by annoyance.

"No, I don't. I think it's fine. It's a lovely dress. The

length is obviously fine with the studio. They sent it to me."

"Hm. Well, I don't like it. But if you don't care about my opinion...." He was in one of his moods again. And Laura was getting tired of it.

"Of course I care about your opinion. But I'm wearing the dress. I'll see you later tonight."

"Are you sure you're not allowed to bring anyone, even your fiancé?"

Ah, so that was his problem. Dylan felt left out. He'd said before that he wanted to go to the taping with her. But she'd asked, and the answer was a firm no. They had very limited space, and all the seats were spoken for. Truthfully, Laura didn't mind. Sometimes it felt a bit smothering to have Dylan hovering around her as much as he did.

"I'm sorry. I did check." She gave him a peck on the lips and grabbed her purse as she opened the front door and waited for him to leave before pulling it shut behind her.

THE DRIVE to the TV studio didn't take too long. Laura had been looking forward to it all week. She'd been shocked and flattered when Harry called a few weeks ago to say that his good friend was one of the executive producers on the New Voices show and he wanted to know if she'd be interested in being one of the guest coaches.

"Really? They want me? I'm so new myself," she'd said when he raised the idea.

"That's why they want you. They have a mix of guest coaches, and they always have one guest coach who is very new and seeing success. That's you. And a bonus, you'll get to perform. I don't think I need to tell you how good that could be for your sales?"

"I'd be honored to do it."

All Laura knew was that she was assigned to be Gary Jones's guest coach. As the most senior coach, they liked the idea of giving him someone new and fresh. When Laura arrived at the studio, she was greeted by a young woman around her own age, who introduced herself as Amelia.

"I'm one of the show coordinators. If you follow me, I'll bring you in to see Gary."

Laura followed her down a long, winding hallway and to a large studio room. She recognized Gary Jones. He rose when he saw her.

"Welcome to the team! I'm a fan already. The show sent me your CD. I understand you wrote most of the songs yourself?"

Laura nodded. "Thank you. Yes, I wrote all of them, actually."

Gary grinned. "Excellent! Okay, so let me fill you in on how this is going to go..."

He gave her the lay of the land and said each contestant would come in one at a time and they already had their songs chosen. Both she and Gary would work with them to help coach them to do the best job possible. Gary was down to eight contestants on his team and one by one, they came in and the day flew. Laura loved every minute of it. She tried to make each contestant feel at ease and pointed out their strengths and made suggestions for what they might change a little to improve their performance.

They were hesitant at first but by the end of each session, they were all feeling more confident. A few had expressed how inspiring it was that Laura was their coach.

"This gives me hope, that anything is possible. You're so new and yet doing so well. I hope to follow in your footsteps," Gina, one of the contestants gushed when they finished. She was talented too, they all were.

"I hope you do. You're doing a great job," Laura encouraged her.

She left, and Gary waved in the next artist.

"This is our last one. Laura Scott, meet Cole Dawson."

Laura looked up, and her jaw dropped when she saw the gorgeous blonde guy from the bar standing before her. The one who thought he knew her. Cole Dawson. Why did that name sound familiar?"

"It's nice to see you again," she said as he shook her hand. His touch gave her what felt like an electrical shock and she pulled her hand away quickly. He looked just as surprised to see her. But Laura knew that they didn't tell the contestants who the guest coaches were going to be. They liked to catch their reactions on air. Cole had turned pale as a ghost which was an interesting reaction. Everyone else had been much more enthusiastic. Maybe he was just nervous. Laura could certainly sympathize with that.

"Cole's father is the Governor of South Carolina," Gary said.

"Oh, how nice." Maybe that was why his name seemed somewhat familiar. She smiled to try to put him at ease. "I didn't know you were a singer, too."

"Do you two know each other?" Gary looked confused.

"We met at one of my shows recently. Just chatted for a quick minute at the bar."

"That's right," Cole said.

"So, let's get started, shall we?" Gary flipped the switch to start the music that they had chosen. Cole went to the microphone and launched into his song. His voice was clear and strong, and Laura felt chills as he sang. Something about the sound of his voice touched her deeply. And seemed oddly familiar. She wondered if she'd heard him sing somewhere before. She knew that some of the artists on the show had recorded music before, toured even, but their careers hadn't taken off yet.

Something came to her, but it was fleeting. She tried to focus on what she'd been thinking of, but her mind was a blank. The harder she tried to recall what it was the more her head started to throb. She felt a wave of nausea roll over her and then broke into a sweat. A migraine was coming. She hadn't had one in years, not since just after the accident, but she knew the signs. She closed her eyes for a moment and tried to calm her mind.

"Laura, are you okay?" Gary sounded concerned.

She opened her eyes. Both Gary and Cole were watching her. She smiled to assure them that she was all right.

"I'm fine. Just a headache, maybe a migraine. I haven't had one in a long time, but I used to get them often."

"I have some Advil in my truck if that might help?" Gary offered.

"Sure, that would be great. If it's not too much trouble."

"None at all. Be back in a flash." He left the room, and Laura sat down and put her hands on her temples.

"I'm sorry you're not feeling well," Cole said. "Maybe my singing made you sick?" His tone was light and teasing.

Laura smiled. "Very funny. You were great, actually, and I've always loved that song." She was quiet for a moment and then said, "I do have one suggestion. When you sing that last line, I'd go softer just before and then give it your all at the end. It will let you end with a really big moment."

He nodded. "Thanks. I will do that. I actually used to do it that way, years ago. My girlfriend at the time made the same suggestion. And it worked. But over the years— you know how it is, you try different things."

"I do know. I've changed the first song I wrote more than any other. I can't seem to resist tinkering with it. It's recorded now, but I still change it up sometimes a little when I sing it live."

"Is that your Young Love song?"

"Yes. You probably heard me sing it that night at the bar."

"I did, and I remember you saying it was your first song." He came and sat down in a folding chair a few feet away from her.

"What's the history of that song? Is there any special meaning to it?"

Laura laughed. "It sounds like there is, doesn't it? But I honestly don't know where that song came from. I was never even interested in music until I was in a serious car accident. I had some memory loss, pretty severe actually," she admitted. "But I don't remember ever having any musical interest or ability until after the accident when I started working in a music shop. The owner taught me to play guitar and suggested I try to write a song. And that was my first attempt."

Cole looked impressed. "That's a hell of a first attempt. It seems like you were meant to do this."

Laura started to smile and then winced with pain and pressed a hand to her forehead. "Sorry, I don't know where this is coming from. I haven't had a headache this bad in years. I thought I was over them, actually."

Gary walked back into the room with a glass of water and a bottle of Advil. He handed both to Laura.

"Thank you." She took two pills and washed them down with the water. Already she felt the tension in her head relax a little. She was glad they were done for the day, and she could go home and rest for a while. She'd call Dylan on the way and let him know she wasn't up for doing anything except going to bed, alone.

Gary turned his attention to Cole. "Great job with that song. Show up and do it just like that and I'm confident we'll be here again next week."

"I hope so. Thanks to both of you. Laura, I'll see you tomorrow. I hope you feel better."

"Thank you. I'm sure I will."

COLE WATCHED as Laura walked out of the building. The past hour and a half had been amazing and disturbing at the time.

"I could really use a beer right now," he muttered to himself.

"I'll go for a beer with you? Where do you want to go?" Gina surprised him by saying. He hadn't realized she was right behind him.

He looked at his cell phone. It was a quarter past five, not too early for a beer. And maybe a burger, too.

"There's a pub around the corner that has good burgers and draft beer. I was thinking of stopping in for dinner. You're welcome to join me." He was happy for the company. It was better than sitting alone at a bar or in his small hotel room. Gina was a sweet girl, but she was smiling kind of funny, and Cole recognized the look. She was interested. Crap. He didn't want to give her the wrong idea, so he looked around and saw one of the other guys he'd gotten to know coming towards them.

"Hey, Kevin, we're going to go grab a beer and something to eat, want to join us?"

"Sure, I'm starving. Lead the way."

Cole drove down the street to the pub, and the others followed close behind. They ordered burgers and a round of draft beers. By the time they finished, Cole was glad to see that Kevin and Gina seemed to be hitting it off. While the two of them gabbed, Cole ordered a second round of beers and couldn't stop thinking about Laura.

He wanted so badly to tell her who they were to each other, but it didn't seem right. He was married, and she was engaged, and he didn't want to upset her. As it was, he was concerned about her headache. Especially as she'd mentioned having them when she was trying to force her memory. What would happen if he filled in the blanks and then her mind took over? He didn't want to hurt her any more than she'd already been hurt.

Both Gina and Kevin were on Gary's team, too, and during the weeks they'd been living and filming in Nashville, they'd all spent a fair bit of time together and had grown close. They were both talented country singers, too. He hoped that they'd stay in touch and maybe cross paths again, maybe even work together at some point. Gary had told him that when he was starting out, there was a small group of guys he'd been close with and they'd collaborate on songs all the time, working together to find the perfect words and melodies. Not for the first time, he wished he could convince Chelsea to move to Nashville. It was the heart of country music, and the energy here was incredible. But he knew she'd never go for it. She'd made that very clear.

When she'd called earlier, she'd asked how much longer he'd be there and when he thought he might be coming home. That's how little attention she paid to the whole process. He reminded her that it depended on how he did tomorrow night. He might be coming home in a day, or here for another week. She promised to watch and surprised him by saying she hoped he'd do well enough to stick around a while longer. He was glad to hear that she was feeling better, too, and keeping busy going out with friends.

"Laura's so awesome. She said she'll be there tomorrow too, to cheer us on," Gina said.

"Yeah, I was surprised by how helpful she was. You know, since she's so new herself. But she had some great suggestions for me. I'm feeling pretty good about my chances," Kevin said.

"She had some good suggestions for me, too," Cole said. When they were dating, Laura's advice was always spot on, and when he took it, it made his performance better. He smiled, remembering that the advice she'd given him earlier that day was the very same suggestions she'd made years ago. Maybe her musical ability had always been in her and they'd just never realized it.

CHAPTER 20

"Don't be nervous. You're going to do great." Laura gave his arm a squeeze and Cole jumped a little at her touch. It was unexpected and still had the same reaction it always did. All of his senses seemed to come alive when Laura was around. He took a deep breath and found himself relaxing. She'd always had a calming effect on him.

"Thanks. I am a little nervous. Big stakes, you know?"

"You've got this. I promise."

He replayed her words to himself as he took his place in the on-deck circle and waited to be announced. They had a live audience now, and the energy in the room was high. When Cole's name was called, he walked out on stage as the music began. Laura's quiet encouragement helped him to focus. He thought back to what Gary had said, too, and he felt something shift inside him as he started to believe. He stood taller, took in the energy all around him and began to sing.

When he finished, there was silence at first, and then an eruption of applause and cheers. Three of the judges stood again for him, and all had nice things to stay. It was all a blur as the lights blocked out much of the audience. Cole looked for Laura and found her in the front row, by the judges. She'd been backstage earlier and must have slipped into her seat when he started to sing. She did that for all the contestants on Gary's team to give them an extra dose of support right before they walked on stage. He waved to her before he walked off stage and joined the others in their row along the side.

They wouldn't get the results until the next day. The live shows allowed for the audience to vote and to buy the songs online. The votes and sales totals all factored into deciding who stayed and who went home. Cole, Gina, and Kevin all did well, and everyone wanted to go out and hear some live music. They all agreed to meet up at seven.

Gary and one of the other judges joined them, too. Cole was pleasantly surprised to see Laura walk in a half hour or so after they arrived. She was with Dylan, her fiancé, who Cole had taken an immediate dislike to the first time they'd met. The feeling seemed to be mutual as Dylan did not look happy when Laura slid into the empty seat next to Cole.

As soon as they ordered their drinks, Dylan leaned back in his seat and put his arm around Laura, resting his hand on her shoulder possessively. Cole noticed that Laura shifted immediately, almost as if she was annoyed by the presence of his hand there, but she allowed it to stay. Cole had to fight the urge to remove it.

"So, you did really great!" Laura said to Cole and then to Kevin and Gina added, "You both did, too. I'm proud of all of you."

"How did you get discovered?" Gina asked. "I heard it was like overnight?"

Laura laughed. "Not quite. It was well over a year. I moved to Nashville with a friend from college and worked as an elementary teacher during the day. And in my spare time, I'd write music and go to writer's nights all over the city." Gina looked confused, so she added, "It's like an open mic night. Lots of places allow new artists to perform. It's a great way to get feedback on your stuff and keep refining it."

"Is that how you got noticed?" Cole asked her.

"Pretty much. I never planned on singing. I came here to be a songwriter only. But the only way to show people my songs was to sing them. The people at Black Duck liked a few of my songs, but they wanted me to sing them."

"Is it true that you wrote all the songs on your album?" Kevin asked.

"It is. And I have some fun news to share with you guys, too."

Everyone leaned in to hear Laura's news, including Dylan who looked surprised.

"I got word just before I came out tonight that two of my songs have been sold to other artists."

"That's so amazing. Can you say to who?" Gina asked.

"I think so. Please keep it to yourself, though, in case I'm not supposed to say anything. It's Blake Shelton and Carrie Underwood."

"Wow," Cole said.

Laura squeezed his arm and laughed. "I know!"

Dylan, meanwhile, was glaring at Laura. "You didn't tell me." His voice was low. Cole could tell he was pissed.

"I'm sorry. I was about to but got another call right before we left. I just found out!"

The band came on, and they spent the next few hours listening to live music, and except for Dylan, who still seemed annoyed at the world, they all had a great time.

"Good luck tomorrow, everyone. I'll see you at the studio," Laura said before they left.

It was going to be a big day. There would be another major cut that would leave just five contestants remaining for the final episode. Odds were not good that Cole, Gina, and Kevin would all make it.

DYLAN WAS UNUSUALLY quiet on the drive home. Laura's few attempts at conversation were met with grumpy, one-word answers. By the time they arrived at her apartment, she was looking forward to falling into bed, alone. She assumed that Dylan was going to go straight home as he'd barely spoken to her, but when they got out of the car, he started walking toward her door. Laura stopped and faced him.

"You don't have to see me inside. Thank you, though."

He looked irritated. "I thought I'd be staying with you tonight."

Laura sighed with frustration. "Why would you think that? You've been a grouch all night. I've had enough of it."

"You should have told me your news first." So, he was still mad about that. "And you shouldn't be hanging out with those newbies. They can't do anything for you. You're way past their level."

"You really think that? That's disappointing, Dylan. They're nice people. I'm happy to try to encourage them. There's room for all of us in this business."

"You're naïve," he spat out.

"I may be, but you're not who I thought you were if that's how you really feel. I think you should go."

"I'm your fiancé. I love you." He ran a hand through his hair, and his eyes pleaded with Laura to let him stay. But she just wanted to get away and be alone.

"We'll talk tomorrow. Good night, Dylan." Laura turned, walked toward her apartment and didn't look back. Once she was inside, she locked the door behind her, changed into her pajamas and climbed into bed. The evening had ended on a sour note and confirmed to Laura that she and Dylan were moving much too fast. He'd pushed her again earlier about setting a date, and she'd felt that same sense of dread. She just wasn't ready to make that commitment. And now her headache was back. She tried to think happy thoughts, willing it to go away and not turn into a migraine. As soon as it eased up a bit, she drifted into a deep sleep.

WHEN SHE WOKE the next morning, she felt unusually tired and was tempted to roll over and go back to sleep, but she had a busy day ahead. Her dreams had been so vivid and confusing because Cole was in them. Only Cole and no one else. They were singing together, and there were other random images that morphed together as dreams often did—the two of them walking along a cute street lined with shops, eating ice cream, sitting in a park. It was all very sweet and peaceful, and throughout the dreams, Laura felt a happy sense of contentment.

She'd never had a dream like that about Dylan, or anyone else she'd dated. The only thing she could figure to explain it was that she and Cole had struck up a nice friendship. She knew he was married, and he knew she was engaged so there was no undercurrent of anything else there. She couldn't help but wonder if it was her subconscious's way of telling her to slow things down with Dylan. Getting engaged was a big step and she needed to be very sure of their relationship before setting a date to get married.

CHAPTER 21

Filming the results show was always stressful for the contestants. Much more so than the day before when they had to perform. It didn't help that the show always wanted to maximize the drama and draw it out so the viewers would watch for the full hour. Each time a name was to be mentioned of who made the cut, they all had to march out on stage and wait, hoping that their name would be called. Only five people would be going on to the final show the following week. And at this point in the process, everyone was a real contender.

Cole was happy for Gina when hers was the first name called. But then the rest of the hour dragged. Almost forty-five minutes passed before they got to the last name, and Cole still hadn't been called. He resigned himself to the fact that it was probably over for him and he'd be heading home. Kevin was by his side, still waiting, too.

"And our last artist that will be going on to the finals is....Cole Dawson!"

Cole had held his breath, waiting for the news and held it a few seconds longer before he relaxed and started breathing again. He'd made it. Kevin hugged him to show his congratulations and Cole wished him good luck. They both promised to keep in touch. The show ended as Cole walked off stage toward the others who were finalists.

Gary and Laura both came over and congratulated him. Gary shook his hand and Laura gave him a cheerful hug. "I'm so proud of you!"

"Thank you. I can't believe it. I'm thrilled."

"You should be. We'll work on picking a song that you can really crush," Gary said.

Laura nodded in agreement, and a thought occurred to Cole. He didn't know if it was possible, but if it was, he knew the perfect song.

"Would you ever consider letting me sing Young Love? It's a great song. It might be cool to have a guy put his spin on it?"

"That's an intriguing idea," Gary said. "What do you think, Laura?"

Laura grinned. "I'm honored, and I love the idea! It's totally fine by me, but let me just check with Black Duck to make sure it's okay."

Cole's cell phone buzzed in his back pocket. He'd set the phone on silent during the show. He pulled it out and saw a text message from his father.

"There's been an accident. Chelsea is in the hospital. Come home ASAP."

COLE CALLED his father as he drove home and learned that Chelsea had been horseback riding and was thrown from her horse. She fractured a rib and badly bruised her whole right side, especially her hip, but there were no other broken bones. He was relieved to hear that she was okay.

"I'm on my way now. Could you let her know I'll be there as soon as I can?"

"I sure will."

"Right. I should go."

"Drive safe."

Cole ended the call and stared out the window at the long stretch of road ahead. He had about eight hours of driving and wouldn't get to Charleston until after dark. Who did Chelsea go horseback riding with? As far as he knew, none of their friends had horses.

CHELSEA WAS asleep when he arrived at the hospital. The doctor was gone for the day, but her nurse filled him in.

"She fell asleep about twenty minutes ago, after her last dose of pain medicine. She should be able to go home in the morning. There's nothing much to do for a fractured rib other than rest." Cole settled into the chair by her bed and waited for her to wake up. When she didn't stir, he eventually closed his eyes and fell asleep himself.

The next morning, he woke with a stiff neck to see Chelsea watching him.

"You came quickly. I wasn't sure if you would."

"Of course I did. I'm glad you're all right."

Chelsea turned and winced from the pain. "I'm pretty banged up."

"I can see that. My father told me too. I'm so sorry."

Chelsea sighed. "I haven't ridden in a while."

"Who were you with?"

"Austin Radley, a guy I work with. He just moved, acquired several horses and wanted to take me riding. I used to ride all the time. It sounded fun, and I've never fallen before."

Cole knew that Chelsea used to ride a lot when she was younger. This was the first he'd heard mention of Austin Radley, though. He wondered if he was the co-worker Chelsea had been talking to the morning he left for Nashville.

"So, are you ready to go home, young lady?" The doctor, an older man who looked to be in his early sixties, stood in the doorway with a clipboard and a stack of forms.

"Yes, I'm ready."

"All right, let's get you out of here."

An hour later, Cole pulled into their driveway and helped Chelsea inside and got her settled on the living room sofa with a few soft blankets, and a cup of tea. They'd stopped at the pharmacy on the way home and picked up a prescription for a pain med, too. Chelsea took one as soon as they got home and before long was dozing on the sofa.

While she was sleeping, Cole called the show producer and told him he'd be back the next day. While Chelsea was sleeping, he went to the grocery store and stocked up on things that would be easy for her to make, canned soups, bags of salad, bread and cold cuts and lots of fluids. She woke around one and Cole fixed her a bowl of chicken noodle soup and a grilled cheese sandwich, which was about the extent of cooking skills. They shared the meal together. Then he broke the news that he'd be heading back to Nashville shortly.

"You're leaving so soon? Who will take care of me?"

Cole sighed. "I'm sorry that you're sore, but you're fine otherwise. I stocked the kitchen for you. You don't have to leave the house if you don't want to. And I called your mother. She's bringing you a home-cooked dinner tonight."

But Chelsea was still pouting. "All you care about is that stupid show."

Cole sighed. "I made the finals. Do you have any idea how important that is to me? It could open all kinds of doors."

"I never thought you'd really go through with it. I thought you'd be a lawyer and work for your father. That would be an amazing job."

And it would reflect well on Chelsea.

"Law school is a backup plan. I've always told you that. This show is a huge deal for me."

They were both silent for a moment.

"Do you want me to call any of your other friends to come visit?" he finally said. Maybe some company would cheer her up.

The shift in conversation seemed to surprise Chelsea. "Yeah, why don't you call….Oh, never mind." She looked away, and a prickly sense of unease crawled up Cole's spine.

"What did you almost say? Who do you want me to call?"

"Oh, no one. I was thinking of Patty, but remembered she's away this week. My mind is just fuzzy from the pain meds. I think it's actually time for me to take another one." She reached for the bottle while Cole cleared the dishes. Once she was settled back on the sofa, he packed his bag and hit the road back to Nashville.

CHAPTER 22

L aura found herself with a free afternoon after filming at the show wrapped up earlier than expected. Her first inclination was to spend the time working on a new song, but after sitting in her living room for an hour feeling nothing but stuck, she decided to do what she usually did when nothing was coming to her. She grabbed her notebook and purse, and walked down the street to the little coffee shop that she used to visit regularly. It was almost three, which was a quiet time and there was no line at the counter. She ordered her usual coffee and took it to a small table by the window.

Something about getting out of the house and just walking or even driving always seemed to open the channel to her mind and got the ideas flowing again. She could barely keep up with her thoughts as she scribbled words down and replayed melodies in her mind. And she had the familiar, addicting buzz when she knew she was on to a good one. When she finally stopped for a moment, after getting everything down and going over it all several times to make sure it was all there the way she wanted it, she took a sip of her coffee and almost laughed. It was stone cold. She glanced at the counter, wondering if she should bother to get another one when she saw a familiar face, two tables down.

"Hey, there. I didn't want to interrupt you earlier. I could tell you were deep in the zone."

Laura got up and gave Jason a big hug. His hair was longer, and he looked as though he needed a good shave, but she didn't care. It was great to see him.

"It's been way too long. How are you? And Janet?"

"We're good. We've been getting a kick out of watching you on New Voices. That's a nice little gig."

Laura pulled up a chair and sat at Jason's table. "It really is. I'm having a lot of fun with it."

"And how's Dylan? Have you guys set a date yet?"

Laura frowned. "He's good. And no we haven't set a date yet."

"Do I sense trouble in paradise?" Laura knew that Jason had never been a big fan of Dylan.

"To be honest, he surprised me with the proposal. I wasn't really there yet. It seemed, still seems, a little fast. So that's why we haven't set a date yet. I don't want to rush it."

Jason nodded. "That's smart. Getting married is huge. You want to be really sure."

He hesitated, as if he wanted to say something but wasn't sure if he should. Laura put her hand on his arm.

"What is it? I know you were never overly fond of him. I do value your opinion."

"He's not a bad guy. It's just that I don't like the way he is with you."

"What do you mean?"

"I know he's a little older, but he talks down to you sometimes and seems bossy and impatient. I just think you deserve better than that."

Laura nodded. "He is moody. And what you're saying—well, I didn't really see it at first. I liked that he was confident and sure of himself. But I can see how that might be perceived differently. Anyway, like I said, we're not rushing into anything."

"I just want you to be happy. Things are finally going so well for you with your career now."

Laura gave his arm a squeeze. "And I love you for it."

"So, which contestant are you rooting for?" Jason asked.

Laura laughed. "Honestly, I like them all."

"They're all good," Jason agreed. "But you must have a favorite?"

"Okay, I do have a soft spot for Cole. His voice is really special. And he may even sing one of my songs. I'm just waiting to hear back from Black Duck to see if they'll allow it. Harry's been out of town.

"Oh, yeah? Which song?" Jason sounded intrigued.

"Young Love."

"Really? I'm surprised you'd consider letting someone else sing that one."

Laura smiled. "I know. But when he suggested it, it just felt right."

IT WAS great to see Jason. When they left, they promised to try to get everyone together soon for a night out. When Laura walked in the door, her cell phone rang, and she could see that it was Black Duck calling.

"Laura, Harry here. I got a message that you want someone to sing Young Love on New Voices?"

"Yeah, do you think it might be possible?"

"Are you kidding? Absolutely. That's free advertising for you and for us. Great idea. Who's going to sing it? That Gina girl or maybe Kristen?"

"No, a guy, actually. Cole Dawson."

There was a moment of silence then Harry said, "No kidding? I'll have to make sure to tune in to see what he does with it. So, are you ready for some more good news?" Harry was always enthusiastic, but he sounded unusually excited, even for him.

"Of course, what is it?"

"How would you feel about going on tour with Miranda Lambert?"

"Miranda Lambert?" Laura was dumb struck.

"Yes, Miranda. Just saw her this past weekend and it turns out she's a fan. She asked if you'd be interested in being one of her two opening acts when she goes on tour next year.

"That would be beyond amazing."

"I'll give Rick a heads up that her people will be calling and he can handle the details for you."

"Thank you, Harry. I just don't even know what else to say. I'm stunned."

He laughed. "Hold on, young lady, you are in for quite a ride! All right, gotta go. Talk soon!"

LAURA WAS TIRED the next day when she arrived at the set for the rehearsals. She'd called Gary the day before and gave him the heads up that Cole had permission to sing her song. She hadn't slept well again. Dylan had come over, and they'd had a quiet night in—a nice night, actually. He'd seemed happy for her news about opening for Miranda Lambert, and they'd gone to bed relatively early. But then, she'd had the most confusing dreams again, and Cole was in most of them.

He was just there, all around her, and they both looked younger and happy. So happy. But when she woke up, she felt a heavy sense of loss. She didn't know what to make of it. The only time she ever dreamed much was when she was stressed about something, and the only thing that was stressing her out lately was her relationship with Dylan. Yet, he wasn't in her dreams at all.

Cole and Gary were already in the studio, talking to a couple of the sound guys about the music when she arrived. Laura took her seat next to Gary and took a sip of the coffee she'd picked up along the way.

"All right, let's see what he does with it," Gary said as

Cole nodded that he was ready to go. The familiar music started, and Cole began to sing. It was an odd sensation for Laura to hear someone else sing her words, especially that song. But Cole sounded as though he'd been singing it for ages. There was so much raw emotion in his voice that it took her by surprise. She hadn't seen him this vulnerable before. The rich tones were there as well, and this tenderness was so appealing. It really worked for the song.

She glanced at Gary. He was smiling. She closed her eyes and let the sound of Cole's voice and her words wash over her and then suddenly froze as images flashed into her mind, similar to the dreams she'd been having but more clear. With a shock, she realized that her dreams about Cole were actually memories.

She didn't fully understand them yet, but she knew that when they first met and Cole said that he knew her, he really did. She was tempted to pull him aside and talk to him about it but decided to wait until after his performance tomorrow. Now that her memory seemed to be coming back a little, she wanted to see if she if might remember more on her own first.

WHEN COLE ARRIVED at the studio that morning, he'd been happy to learn that he had approval to sing Laura's song. He felt in his gut that it was important for him to sing it, for some reason. He was surprised by how raw he sounded at certain points. His voice cracked a few times, but he knew it was in a way that would be appealing to the listeners, especially the female ones who he hoped would feel the aching and longing in his voice for the young lovers that had been split apart. He'd been singing directly to Laura, and he'd noticed her expression change half-way through the song. She seemed to go inside herself, though her foot was still tapping along to the beat and she was smiling. When he stopped singing, both Laura and Gary stood and clapped.

"That was really special," Laura said.

"Thank you. It's a special song."

Gary laughed. "You did a good job, but let's make it great. Try it again, but at the end of the first chorus, why don't you hold that last note a bit longer? You could really have a moment with this one. The girls are going to go crazy."

They went through the song a few more times. Cole noticed that each time, Laura watched intently but had fewer comments than usual and at times seemed far away. By the time they finished, it was noon and everyone was starving. Gina wanted to go back to the pub for lunch, and that sounded good to Cole, too. He was too keyed up to just go back to his hotel room. He knew he'd barely sleep as it was. He needed to keep busy and not think too much about tomorrow so he could get to sleep early.

"Where are you guys going for lunch? Mind if I tag along?" Laura asked.

"Of course," both Gina and Cole said at the same time.

Cole and Laura ordered sodas and burgers. Gina had a beer and salad. Their waitress, Lisa, was a cheerful older woman who had them laughing.

"I sure as hell don't miss waitressing," Gina said when Lisa went to take another order. "If I manage to win tomorrow, I will never waitress again. Mark my words!"

"It really is hard work," Laura agreed.

"Oh, did you waitress, too?" Gina asked.

"No, I never have, but I know people who have. It's not easy." Laura smiled, but it was a sad smile, and she put her hand to her head as if it hurt.

"Hey, are you okay? You look a little pale." Cole was concerned as she really didn't seem herself.

"I'm fine, just a little light-headed for a minute. I'll be fine once I eat. I missed breakfast this morning." Laura was unusually quiet, but once their food arrived and she began to eat, she seemed herself again.

When they finished eating, they went their separate ways and when Cole got back to his hotel, he decided to go for a run. He needed to burn off some nervous energy so there'd be a small chance he could actually fall asleep and get some rest before the biggest day of his life.

CHAPTER 23

When Laura got home, the first thing she did was to call Dylan and tell him she wasn't feeling up to doing anything. She needed to be alone. All she felt like doing was making a cup of hot tea, wrapping herself in a soft fleece blanket and burrowing into her squishy living room sofa. Her head was throbbing as she alternated between wanting the images and memories to become more clear to wishing they'd just stop. It was overwhelming.

A profound sense of sadness came over her again as she thought back to her comment at the pub about knowing how hard waitresses work. She had no idea where that came from, but it had brought waves of love and sadness at the same time, and her eyes felt damp as she tried to make sense of it. It was out there but beyond the reach of understanding.

Just as her eyes grew heavy, her phone dinged that she had a new email. She sleepily picked up the phone and read the message. It was a forwarded email from Sami, the marketing assistant at Black Duck. Someone had emailed her through the Facebook page they'd set up, a Barbara Lynch, who said she'd graduated high school with Laura, in Charleston. A sharp pain raced across Laura's temples as she re-read the message. Barbara said she'd lived a few doors down from where Laura and her mother had lived, and she just wanted to say hello and tell her how much she'd enjoyed hearing her on the radio. At the top of the note, Sami had written, "I thought you should see this and I just wanted to double-check. Did you grow up in Charleston? I'd thought it was Montana. Thanks!"

The sadness swept over her again, and this time it was crippling. The tears flowed as the first clear image of her mother appeared. Laura saw her sweet face, wavy blonde hair and the waitress uniform she was wearing as she sat on her patio, smoking a cigarette and drinking a glass of white wine. She cried for what felt like forever, and when the tears finally slowed, the last thought she had before she fell into a dead sleep, was why had Aunt Helen lied to her?

WHEN LAURA WOKE in the morning, she felt like she'd been run over by a truck. Every part of her body ached with sadness and confusion. She'd had more dreams with Cole in them and her mother, but she still fully didn't understand where Cole fit in. She called her aunt as soon as she'd had her first cup of coffee. It was very early in

Montana, a little before seven, but Aunt Helen was an early riser and Laura knew that she'd be up.

"Hi, honey. This is a nice surprise! Is everything okay?" Her aunt sounded happy to hear from her and a little concerned that she was calling so early.

"No, everything is not okay. I met someone in Nashville that said he knows me and I've been dreaming a lot. I'm starting to remember things, finally."

There was a long moment of silence before Aunt Helen softly asked, "What have you remembered?"

"My mother. She died in the accident, didn't she? Not when I was little." When Laura woke that much was clear to her, but she still didn't remember the accident itself.

"She did. I'm really sorry, honey."

"Why did you lie to me?"

There was a long, heavy silence, and then a crack in her voice as she said, "I never wanted to. My brother persuaded me that it was for the best for everyone and it was the only way I could get the money to pay for Harold's care."

"You never mentioned a brother. Do I know him?"

Aunt Helen sighed. "I'm afraid that you do. Dalton Dawson."

Laura shivered at the familiar name and then made the connection.

"Cole's father? The governor?"

"Yes, I've been watching the two of you on that show. And wondering if I might get this phone call. What did Cole tell you?"

Laura pressed a hand against her head, which was throbbing again.

"I actually met him before the show, at a bar I was playing at. He said hello and that he knew me, and I told him he must have me mixed up with someone else." Laura then asked the question she needed to know. "Did we date?"

"Yes. You were high school sweethearts, and I believe you were going to get married."

Laura thought about that. It sounded right even though she still couldn't remember it.

"And Cole's father didn't want us to get married, I take it?"

"No. He thought you were both too young. He paid for your college, you know."

"He did? Why would he do that?"

Aunt Helen laughed bitterly. "Why do you think? Because he knew what he was doing was wrong and on some level, he felt guilty about it."

But something still didn't make sense to Laura. "Why did Cole and I break up?"

"Dalton lied to him. He told Cole that he offered you money for a full ride at college if you left him without saying goodbye."

Laura could feel tears welling up again as she tried to process how Cole's father had gone to such extremes to get her out of his son's life. "But why would he do that? He must have really hated me."

"Dalton has made his share of mistakes. This is at the

top of the list. Do you remember where you lived with your mother?"

"No. It hasn't come back to me yet," Laura admitted.

"You lived in a trailer park, and even though Cole said it was a nice one, Dalton was getting ready to run for governor, and he worried about things like that."

"He was a snob."

"Yes, and it was all too much for him—the trailer park, the two of you wanting to get married and...well, it was just too much."

Aunt Helen had been about to say something else. "What else was there?" Laura asked.

"You should really talk to Cole."

Laura could tell by her voice she didn't want to say more and at this point, Laura knew she needed to talk to Cole, anyway. "You're right. I will."

"I'm so very sorry, Laura. I hope—I hope you can forgive me in time. I really did grow to love you like a daughter." Aunt Helen's voice broke, and Laura felt her own tears coming again. She wanted to be furious with this woman who wasn't even her aunt, but she still felt like the only family that she had left.

"I have to go."

She ended the call and collapsed on the sofa again, closing her eyes and trying to process it all. She felt like she could crawl back into bed, cry a little and then sleep all day. It was so tempting. But she knew she had to get moving. And that keeping busy would help to keep her mind off everything.

Something was different about Laura. Cole noticed it instantly when she walked backstage just before the show and wished him luck. She seemed paler and almost fragile.

"Are you feeling okay?" he asked after they'd chatted for a few minutes.

"I'm great! Excited to cheer you on." She smiled enthusiastically, but something seemed off. Her smile didn't quite reach her eyes.

"I can't thank you enough for all of your help and for letting me do your song. At least I know I'll be putting my best foot forward."

"And if it's meant to be, it will be," Laura said.

Cole did a double-take at her words. She used to always say that—or rather her mother did and Laura picked it up from her. A wave of sadness came over him. He really missed the connection that they'd had. They'd always been there for each other. As much as he loved the city, Cole was feeling very alone in Nashville. He'd hoped that maybe Chelsea would surprise him by coming to his final show, but when he talked to her the night before and mentioned the possibility, she'd actually laughed at the thought.

"I'm feeling a little better, but no way am I up for that kind of drive."

He almost mentioned that she could fly, but didn't bother. Obviously, she just didn't want to come.

"All right. I'll see you in a few days, then."

"I'll be here."

Chelsea hung up without even wishing him good luck, which didn't surprise him all that much. She'd made it clear that, like his father, she was tolerating the music thing and eager for him to get it out of his system.

"Cole, they're calling for you to get ready." Laura tapped him on the arm, and he snapped back to attention.

"Thanks. I'll see you after."

Laura took her usual seat in the front row, by the judges. She could tell Cole was nervous and hoped he'd be able to shake it off and focus once he got on stage. She was confident that once he started to sing he'd get into the same zone he was in the day before. If he did, he had a very good shot at winning. Gina was the front-runner, but Cole and the others were popular, too, so it would be close.

The music began, and Cole began to sing. Laura didn't think it was possible, but after a wobble in the first line, he found his rhythm in a way that was mesmerizing and even better than before. She felt as though he was singing right to her and several times, their eyes locked. Goosebumps ran down her arms as he sang and a new image came to her, of the two of them sitting in a park by a tree, eating ice cream. Cole was carving something on a tree, but it was kind of fuzzy, and she couldn't make out what it said. The feeling she had was one of great joy and contentment, followed by a confusing wave of sadness.

Cole's voice cracked as he sang the final line and his

eyes locked onto hers again, and as he finished, he smiled. Laura knew it was meant for her and she was the first one on her feet to clap when he finished. The crowd went crazy and when the applause finally died down, Mike, the host, asked him how he felt.

"I feel great. It's an awesome song."

"It seemed very emotional for you. Does this song have any special meaning for you?"

Cole hesitated. He looked Laura's way for a split-second. So quickly that Laura doubted anyone but her would notice.

"It does, actually. It reminds me of my first love, my high school sweetheart."

"And what was her name?"

Laura held her breath, waiting for his answer.

"Her name was Laura."

"Well, there you go. It seems like it was meant to be for you to sing this song. Good luck, Cole!"

WHEN THE SHOW wrapped a few minutes later, there was a lot of enthusiastic activity backstage. Laura guessed that most of the contestants would be going out for a celebratory drink. She wanted to try to grab a few minutes alone with Cole before he left to join the others as she wouldn't be going with them. She had plans for dinner with Dylan, and he'd checked in several times by text message.

"Cole, do you have a minute?" Laura asked as Gina walked towards the door with several others.

"Of course." He looked happy to see her and Laura knew he was still riding high after a great performance. A steady stream of people had stopped by to congratulate him.

Laura led him into an empty room and sat in one of several chairs that were around a coffee table.

"I know when we first met, at that bar where I was performing, you mentioned that you knew me. I thought you were mistaken, that you had me mixed up with someone else, but now I'm not so sure. About anything."

He looked at her intently. "Are you starting to remember?"

She nodded. "It's all really hazy. But it's coming back slowly." Laura felt a rush of emotion and tears welling up as she said, "I forgot my own mother. How could that be?"

Cole reached over and took her hand, squeezing it softly. "Your mom was awesome."

"You knew her?"

"Yeah. I got to know her pretty well. You and I knew each other well," he said carefully.

Laura nodded. "We dated."

He grinned. "You remember that?"

"Sort of. Bits and pieces, but no details. I remember us sitting in a park by a tree."

"Eating ice cream? That was our spot. I carved our names in that tree."

"We were happy then." It wasn't a question. The image in her mind radiated happiness.

"We were in love. Head over heels. We...were going to get married." A cloud came over his face for a moment.

Laura sensed that he'd been about to say something and had held back.

"We were young to get married?"

"We were. When I first told my father I wanted to marry you, he told me that I was out of my mind and that we were just way too young. We both wanted to go to college, and he wanted us to wait until after we graduated."

"That does seem sensible."

Cole nodded and looked as though he wanted to say something, but was hesitant to do so.

"What is it?" Laura thought she had an idea. When Cole stayed silent, she asked, "Was I pregnant?"

He looked somewhat relieved and then sad at the memory.

"Yes. Once we got over the initial shock, we were both thrilled. A little scared, for sure, but we knew we could make it work. You'd been planning to go to school in Montana, but Clemson had accepted you, too, so you were going to switch and go there instead, with me."

"Your father must have hated that idea."

Cole looked away, and Laura noticed a muscle twitch along his jaw.

"He lost his mind a little."

"Tell me about the accident."

Tears streamed down Laura's face as Cole told her about that day. How they'd been so excited to go see the doctor together. And how her mother had been driving and another car had come out of nowhere and slammed into them.

"It was the worst day of my life," he finished.

After a few minutes, when her tears finally slowed, Laura said, "I talked to your Aunt Helen. She said your father offered me money to leave you. I never even knew that. I'm so sorry that you thought I abandoned you."

"None of this is your fault. I couldn't understand for the longest time how you could have done that. The Laura I knew never cared about money."

She smiled. "I still don't, really. As long as I can pay my bills."

"That was one of the things I always loved about you. My father never understood it. It's all he cares about. We're not on the best of terms now."

"I'm sorry."

"Don't be. He got everything he wanted. He's governor. He even has a new woman in his life, Claire. She's actually really nice. Too good for him. But she's softened him."

"I wouldn't say he got everything he wanted. He doesn't have your respect. He can't be happy about that."

"No, he doesn't have my respect. He is my father, but I don't have much of a relationship with him these days."

"You're married, though. Tell me about your wife, Chelsea?"

"I met Chelsea in college. She's blonde, beautiful, smart and like my father, she's very ambitious and interested in politics. They get along great."

Laura smiled. "And you're happy?"

"Happy enough I guess. We've always had fun, gotten along well. It was actually better before we got married though. I guess it's just the getting used to living with someone. She works long hours, and she doesn't approve of the music stuff at all. She wants me to be a lawyer and work for my dad."

"A lawyer?" Laura couldn't picture him as an attorney. Cole was too casual and laid back. She could see him carrying a guitar, not a briefcase.

"I just graduated from law school. Still need to study for the bar. I do find it interesting, but it's more of a backup plan, in case the music doesn't work out."

"Well, I hope you never need your backup plan."

He smiled. "Me, too. We'll find out soon enough. Maybe I'll be sticking around for a while."

"I hope so!"

"And what about you? Are you happy, Laura? Have you and Dylan set a date?"

Was she happy?

"These past few months have been magical, a whirlwind. Dylan and I haven't been dating all that long. He proposed unexpectedly, and publicly, and it took me by surprise. I'd love it if time slowed down a little. So, no we haven't set a date, and I'm not in a hurry to pick one."

Cole nodded as if he approved.

"I think that's smart. Trust me when I say that marriage isn't something you want to rush into."

"Now that you're back in my life, I hope that we can stay in touch. There's still so much that I don't remember."

"Of course. What's your cell phone number?"

Laura told him, and Cole plugged it into his phone and then tapped out a text message. "There, now we're in each other's phones. Call or text me anytime, for anything. I mean it."

"I will. Thank you." Her phone buzzed and she saw a text message from Dylan, wondering when she'd be home. "I have to run. We have dinner plans tonight. But I'll see you tomorrow. We'll talk more then." They both stood and she gave him a grateful hug. "Thanks, again."

CHAPTER 24

Dylan wasn't happy at first that Laura didn't feel like going out for dinner and preferred to get takeout and stay at home. She just wasn't up to being social in any way. She didn't want to have the conversation over the phone but said she'd fill him in when he came over. And she told him she needed it to be an early night as she was exhausted and couldn't wait to go to bed early.

"What is going on with you? Are you sick or something?" he'd asked.

"No, it's nothing like that."

He arrived with a bag of Thai takeout and Laura opened a couple of beers for them. Over spring rolls and Pad Thai, she filled him in on most of what she'd learned, leaving out the part about being pregnant. Dylan, as expected, was furious at both Cole and his father.

"It's not Cole's fault."

"He must have known what was going on."

"No, he swears he didn't, and I believe him."

"Well, what are you going to do about it? It must be criminal what he did to you. And he's a governor now. Talk about a scandal. He should pay."

"That did cross my mind. I was pretty furious at first. Still am, actually, but I don't think that's going to help the situation any."

Dylan took a big swig of his beer. He looked incredulous.

"Are you kidding me? You need to blow this up. Get that man kicked out of office."

Laura sighed. "I'm looking at the bigger picture. That's not going to help Cole or me. It could hurt us both."

Dylan shook his head in disgust. "That's crazy. I couldn't disagree more. But, it's your choice, of course."

"Thank you."

They ate quietly for a few minutes and then Dylan looked her in the eyes and asked, "And what about Cole? You two seemed close on the show. There's still a connection there. Does he want you back?"

Laura set her fork down. "Don't be ridiculous. That was a long time ago. We were kids. And besides, he's married."

"Right. And we will be soon, too. So, let's set a date. That will send a message just in case he gets any ideas." Dylan's tone was teasing, but his eyes were serious. Laura's head began to ache.

"Dylan, I told you before I'm not ready to set a date. Please don't push me on that, not now."

"Fine."

Laura yawned and looked at the clock. It was early still, but it felt later.

"Am I boring you?"

"No. I'm sorry. I'm just exhausted. It's been a lot all at once. I'm just now dealing with my mother dying. You can't even imagine."

Dylan sighed. "You're right. I'm sorry. I can't begin to imagine."

After they finished eating, Laura put the leftovers away and they watched TV for a little while. Laura couldn't stop yawning, though, so Dylan didn't stay long and as soon as he left, she fell into bed and into a sound sleep.

COLE'S CONVERSATION with Laura and the possibility of winning made sleep near impossible. He didn't expect to win. He knew Gina was considered the front-runner, but he also knew he'd killed it with Laura's song, and he and Gina were neck and neck on the iTunes chart. He was actually one spot ahead of her at the moment, but they kept switching places. And of course, he had no idea about the actual vote. So, winning was a real possibility, and it would be life-changing.

And then there was Laura. He thought he'd feel better when she remembered who he was, but instead, it made him even sadder for what he'd lost, what they'd both lost. But, he reminded himself that they were different people now, older, and both had moved on. He'd married, and she was engaged. He didn't like Dylan, but it's not like his opinion mattered.

Although he wasn't as happy as he'd hoped to be with Chelsea. He'd been talking to her less and less since he'd been in Nashville. When they did talk, the conversations were short, and he always felt like she was anxious to get off the phone and back to whatever it was that she was doing. Maybe it would be better when he got home, and they were able to spend more time together.

When he arrived at the studio, the energy was high, and the five remaining contestants were all a bundle of nerves. They wouldn't know the results until the last few minutes of the show. The remaining time would be filled with guest artists singing whatever new single they were hoping to promote. He knew that Laura was going to be debuting Magic, a song that she was excited about and that he'd heard live the first time he saw her weeks ago. They were coordinating it so that she'd sing it on the show first and then it would get radio airplay right away after that.

Cole saw Laura backstage before the show began. Her song was going to be up first after they announced the name of the first artist to be eliminated.

She smiled when she saw him.

He spoke first. "How are you doing? I can't wait to hear your song."

"I'm okay. A little nervous. Excited, too. How are you doing? My fingers are crossed for you."

"Thanks. I appreciate that. I'm a little nervous, too," he

admitted and then grinned. "Who am I kidding? I've never been this nervous before."

The lights flashed, indicating it was time for everyone to get to their places. Cole rushed to take his seat with the others. When the show started, they had to all go on stage and immediately the first name was called, and Cole couldn't breathe until they called a name that wasn't his, which brought them down to four finalists. They shuffled back to their seats and then Laura was introduced, and she began to sing her new song.

Cole was blown away again, even though he'd heard the song once before. Young Love was amazing and personal, but Magic was big and fun with a catchy melody. He could tell by the crowd's reaction that it was going to be another hit for her. Laura was a star-in-the-making.

The rest of the hour was a blur. Before every commercial break, they brought the finalists out and announced the name of another eliminated artist. Cole held his breath each time and survived until it was just him and Gina left. He really liked Gina, and if he couldn't win, he'd be happy for her. But still, he'd never wanted anything so badly before. He and Gina walked out together and held hands as they announced the winner—and it wasn't him. Gina screamed, and he immediately gave her a big hug while streamers and confetti rained down onto the stage.

Everyone swarmed around Gina as the show ended. His coach, Gary, came over and gave him a big hug.

"You did great. I really thought you had it there for a while. This was a close one, though. You know, sometimes you're better off not winning these things. There might be something else better coming your way instead." He slapped Cole affectionately on the back, took his phone number and promised to keep in touch. "No promises, but I'll see what I can do for you."

"You did so well," Laura said as she gave him a big hug.

"Thanks. Close, but no cigar."

"This is just the beginning, you know. So what that you didn't win? You can still make the most of this opportunity. Is there any way you can move to Nashville? Being here, being seen, meeting people. It makes a difference."

Cole sighed. "I wish. I'd love nothing more. But, Chelsea will never go for it. The most she'll allow is occasional long weekends." And he knew she wouldn't be keen on him leaving again anytime soon. He also knew that the pressure was likely to start again for him to focus on landing an attorney position somewhere. Which wasn't likely to happen either unless he got serious about studying for and passing the bar.

"Well, the next time you come to Nashville, let me know. I'd love to see you and catch up."

"I'd like that. And same to you. If you ever get to Charleston, look me up. Are you sure you're doing okay?" Cole had been so caught up in feeling sorry for himself that he'd forgot to consider how Laura was handling everything.

"I'm okay, really. I just might go to Charleston soon. I think it might help me to get more of my memories back."

Cole nodded. "When you're ready, I think it might be a good idea."

"Have a safe trip back, Cole." Laura pulled him in for a goodbye hug and he breathed in her scent. She smelled the same as he remembered. Like sweetness and light, fresh and clean and just Laura. He would miss her.

CHAPTER 25

Chelsea was still at work when Cole arrived home the next day a little past four. He felt grimy from the long drive and had barely slept the night before. He'd been too keyed up, his mind racing as he thought about having to shift to his Plan B. Even though he'd known it was a long shot, he'd hoped hard that he'd win. It had seemed possible, for a while.

But he'd had a lot of time to think during the drive home and knew he had to be realistic. He'd given it his best shot. Aside from moving to Nashville, which wasn't an option, Cole knew he wasn't likely to get on anyone's radar in Charleston. As much as he hated the thought of it, he knew it was time to suck it up and at least start studying for the bar.

He knew he could start right away at his father's firm, but that was a last resort. Once he passed the bar, he'd have more options, but in the meantime, he could start sending out his resume. There was a good chance someone would hire him as an associate, and he could work and study at the same time. Maybe it wouldn't be so bad. He could still do side gigs with the guys now and then. Plus, he knew that Chelsea was eager for him to get to work soon. She'd made that very clear.

Cole was just toweling his hair after coming out of the shower when he heard her car pull into the driveway. She looked surprised to see him when she walked in.

"I didn't expect you back until tomorrow!" As she smiled and kissed him hello, there was a familiar tenseness about her, and he sensed that she was in one of her moods. She got like that sometimes when everything he said seemed to irritate her, and he could never figure out where it came from or what he'd done. This time, it seemed that she just didn't like the interruption to her schedule.

"I didn't have any reason to stick around. I thought you might be glad to see me. Missing me, even?" he asked in a teasing tone.

She rewarded him with a tight smile. "Of course I am. I just wasn't expecting you back so I made plans to go out with some of the people from work tonight." She checked her cellphone. "We're meeting in an hour. I wanted to jump in the shower and freshen up. You're welcome to join us, of course." Her tone wasn't overly welcoming, though. Cole guessed that she'd probably rather that he didn't join them. He barely knew her co-workers. His first instinct was to tell her to go ahead without him, and to have fun. But he started to feel a bit irritated himself. He'd barely seen her in recent weeks. If it were the other way around, he would have happily canceled his plans with his friends.

"Sure, I'd love to join you all."

Chelsea did a double-take. "Oh, okay. Great. I'll be ready in about twenty minutes."

AN HOUR LATER, Cole ordered a second beer at a crowded, loud bar downtown and wished he'd stayed home. After an initial round of congratulations from Chelsea's co-workers for coming in second on the show, the conversation turned back to their jobs and Cole didn't have much to contribute. Chelsea had introduced him to the half-dozen or so colleagues that were already at a table when they arrived. All of their names went in one ear and out the other, except for one, Austin Radley.

He looked just like his name. Tall and arrogant. Cole disliked him immediately and was annoyed that he and Chelsea were practically finishing each other's sentences.

"You're like an old married couple," Marsha said with a laugh and then looked Cole's way and apologized. "I didn't mean anything by that."

"Oh, Cole understands. I told him Austin, and I have been spending a lot of time together on this project. Austin is my work husband. I've seen more of him than Cole lately!"

"Are you back for good now," Austin asked.

"Yeah, I think so."

"Cole is going to work for his father," Chelsea said, smiling at Cole in a way that dared him to deny it.

"I need to pass the bar first," he said as he reached for his beer.

"Your father would probably let you start working sooner, though," she insisted. "It might be a great idea to get in there and get started."

Cole sighed. "Maybe. We'll see."

Two hours later, everyone headed home. Cole was exhausted from the long day of driving. Chelsea was still chattering non-stop about some project they were working on and how Austin was such a great mentor. Cole yawned and fell into bed as soon as they got home.

HE SPENT the next week cracking the books to study for the bar and hating every minute of it. He didn't hate the law, exactly, but it was a reminder that he'd failed in Nashville and he kept remembering his time there. Everyone lived and breathed music and the past few weeks were the happiest he'd been in a long time. He'd heard Laura on the radio a few times since and each time he heard her voice, he thought about her and wondered how she was doing. He hoped that if she did decide to come to Charleston that she'd call. He'd love to show her around and, selfishly, he wanted her to get her memories back to remember how it had been with them. He wondered if she was happy with Dylan. He hoped so, but there was something that he hadn't liked about the guy. A possessiveness or jealousy that he wouldn't want for Laura. Even if they weren't together, he still wanted her to be happy.

He wished that Chelsea would consider moving to Nashville, or at least closer to it. But she'd made it clear that wasn't an option and now that he was home and the show was done that chapter of his life was over, as far as she was concerned. She'd mentioned working for his father several times this week, pushing for an answer each time. Finally, she managed to get him to agree to dinner at the club after church on Sunday. When his father brought it up over dessert, Chelsea glared at him, and it was just easier to agree to start going into the office the following week.

Cole was quiet on the ride home from the club, dreading the start of his new career. But he had agreed long ago that if the music thing didn't work out, he'd start focusing on law. It seemed like it was time to do that. Chelsea, however, was in a great mood. She reached over and took his hand as he drove and gave it a squeeze.

"It's going to be great working for your father. I just know it."

MONDAY MORNING CAME QUICKLY, and as Cole was walking to the car to drive to his father's office, his cell phone rang. He didn't recognize the number, but the area code was from Nashville. He quickly took the call and said hello.

"Cole Dawson? This is Harry Evans from Black Duck studios. Do you have a minute?"

Cole leaned against his truck. "Yes, of course."

"I didn't follow much of that show you were on, but I did catch your performance of Young Love. I was curious after Laura told me you wanted to sing it. You did a fine job with it."

"Thank you."

"More than fine, actually. Your iTunes single of Young Love is still selling pretty good, and Laura's sales went up too, by having you sing it on national television. It was good for both of you. Which brings me to why I'm calling. Your coach, Gary, and I are working on a new label that he's going to manage. He's picking the artists and will guide the development of their first album. He'd like you to be one of his first artists, if you're interested."

Cole felt lightheaded for a moment, wondering if he'd heard right.

"Of course I'm interested. I'm honored."

"Excellent. Can you make it in sometime this week to sit down with Gary and me and the team? Get your contract signed and get things rolling for you?"

They agreed to meet the next day, late afternoon. Cole grinned stupidly as he ended the call and immediately dialed his father's line.

"Dad, I'm afraid I won't be coming in today, or anytime soon, actually. I'm heading back to Nashville."

CHAPTER 26

By the time Cole checked into his hotel, it was a quarter to six and he knew Chelsea would be just getting home. He knew that she wasn't going to be happy with his news.

"You're in Nashville? I thought you were starting with your father today?" Her tone was icy and confused.

"I was on my way in. But then Black Duck studios called. They're huge, Chelsea, and they want to sign me to a record deal."

"So you just left. Without even talking to me first?"

"There wasn't a whole lot to talk about. This is what I've always wanted. There's no way I could say no."

"I see. So, that's it then? You live in Nashville now?"

"No, of course not. I'll be home in a few days. But I will be spending more time here once we start recording and hopefully performing."

"I'm not happy about this."

Cole felt bad that he didn't tell Chelsea in person. But,

he meant what he'd said. There wasn't anything to talk about and if the way this conversation was going was an indication, it would have been even worse in person.

"I'd hoped you'd be happy for me. You know I've always wanted this."

Chelsea was silent and Cole could feel her fuming. "Chelsea, we'll talk in a few days. We can find a way to make this work."

"I have to go. Someone's on the other line. Bye, Cole."

Chelsea hung up and Cole sighed. It had been a long drive and a tense conversation. He needed to go for a long run, to work off some steam and tire himself out enough that he'd be able to get a good night's sleep.

THE NEXT AFTERNOON, he arrived at Black Duck studios at a quarter to two. He met with Gary and the studio head, Harry Evans, and a team of people whose names went in one ear and out the other.

"We all liked what we heard. We all saw you on the show and I for one am glad you didn't win. Because now we have a chance to work together." Harry looked around the room dramatically and everyone nodded.

"I couldn't say anything to you then," Gary said, "because we hadn't ironed out all the details yet, but you were the first artist on my list. I'm looking to step back from performing myself and do more producing. I think we worked well together on the show and I think this could be amazing."

"I do too. I'm honored that you thought of me."

"So, here's what we're thinking," Harry began. He told Cole what the process would be and asked if he'd written any songs himself.

"A few. I've been playing around a little the past year or so." He knew he was nowhere near Laura's level as a songwriter, though.

"Okay, give Gary whatever you've got. We'll review it all. We have a few other songs in mind for you too. And this is our standard contract. Why don't you review it tonight and if all looks good, drop a signed copy back in the next day or two."

"We can start recording sessions a month from now, if that works for you?" Gary asked.

Cole nodded. "That sounds great."

As they walked out, Harry handed him two business cards. "Here's my contact info, if you need it. You got a manager yet?"

"No, I probably should look into that."

"Rick is Laura's manager. He's a good guy. Feel free to give him a call or ask around. Gary probably knows people too."

"Give Rick a call. If you guys don't click, I have a few other names you can try."

"It may be premature to say it, but welcome aboard, Cole!" Harry slapped him on the back and Gary shook his hand. Both said they looked forward to talking again soon.

Cole was in a daze as he walked to his truck. As soon as he got inside and closed the door, he called Rick and set an appointment to meet the next day. Rick told him to bring the contract with him and before they hung up, he offered his congratulations too. There was one other person that Cole wanted to share his good news with. He looked her number up and Laura answered on the first ring.

"Hi Cole. Are you in Nashville already?"

"I am and I have some really good news. Any chance you might be available for a celebratory drink?"

"Of course. Where are you now?"

He smiled. "I'm just leaving Black Duck studios."

There was a moment of silence and then Laura practically screamed. "Oh, my God, Cole I'm so excited for you! I can't wait to hear all about it. There's a pub right around the corner from there. The Black Rose. I can meet you in about twenty minutes."

WHEN LAURA ARRIVED at the Black Rose, Cole was sitting at the bar and he grinned when he saw her. She gave him a big hug hello and slid onto the stool next to him. The bartender, an older man with gray hair, a pot belly and a friendly smile came right over to take their drink order. They both ordered the local IPA draft beer and as soon as their drinks arrived, Laura lifted hers to toast Cole.

"Congratulations! Now tell me everything."

Cole told her about his afternoon at the studio and what Harry and Gary were thinking.

"They asked me if I've written many songs." Cole looked sheepish. "I mean, I've written some but nothing like what you've done. I guess I need to start working harder at that. They did say they have a few songs in mind for me, though, so that's good."

"I might have a few that could work for you." Laura immediately started to mentally sift through her catalog of songs and began to feel excited. She could think of at least three, maybe four songs that could be well-suited to Cole's voice.

"You don't have to do that. I wasn't hinting. I hope you don't think that I was?"

Laura laughed. "Don't be silly. I literally have hundreds of songs and I would love for you to sing some of them. I'll send you the ones that I have in mind. Hopefully one or two might work."

Cole looked excited by the possibility. "If you could, that would really be awesome."

Laura smiled. "So, when are you thinking about moving here?"

Cole took a sip of his beer and looked deep in thought for a moment. "I don't know that I'll actually be able to move here. I still need to talk this through with Chelsea. It kind of happened suddenly, and she is adamant that she doesn't want to move to Nashville. They want me to start recording in about a month."

Laura felt for him. She knew how badly he wanted to move to Nashville. She couldn't imagine not living there. It was the heart of the country music world.

"Will you go back and forth, then? That might be kind of tough."

"It's not ideal, I know. I'll figure something out."

"Well, I'm excited for you. When I get home tonight,

I'll go through my stuff and I'll get an email off to you tomorrow with a couple of songs. Let me know what you think and then I'll forward the ones you like onto Harry for approval."

Cole looked excited to hear it. "That would be awesome. I can't wait to see them."

Laura's stomach grumbled, and she laughed. "Did you hear that? I haven't had anything to eat since breakfast. Are you hungry?"

"I can always eat. You want to grab a bite? I'll get us some menus."

He got the waitress's attention and after a quick look at the menu, they both ordered barbecued pulled pork sandwiches and fries. It was one of the things Laura had fallen in love with when she moved to Nashville. Tender pulled pork smothered in tangy barbecue sauce. It just wasn't the same in Montana.

While they ate, Laura told him all about where to go in Nashville and all the different venues that she'd played. "Once you're here, I'll introduce you to some folks and show you around. You'll be in heaven with all the really great places to hear music." Laura was excited for Cole and was looking forward to showing him why she loved Nashville so much.

"I'd love that."

Laura's phone rang just as they finished eating and she saw that it was Dylan. She also saw that it was much later than she realized. She and Cole had been chatting for several hours and she'd lost all track of time.

"Where are you?" Dylan sounded tense and irritated when she answered the phone.

Laura hesitated for a moment only because she knew that what she said was likely to irritate him even further. "I'm at the Black Rose pub having a bite to eat with Cole. We're celebrating some good news that he got today."

"You're with Cole? At the Black Rose? I'm at your house waiting for you. I thought we'd have dinner tonight?"

"I didn't think we had dinner plans?" Laura was sure they'd never discussed it.

"No, we didn't," he admitted. "But I usually see you most nights, and I figured you be home."

Laura began to feel irritated as well. "Well, I'm not home. Why don't you come here and have a drink with us?"

"You're kidding right? Are you coming home soon?"

She sighed. "Yeah, I think we'll probably be leaving soon."

"Then I'll see you when you get here."

Cole looked concerned as she set her cell phone down. "I hope things are okay with you and Dylan?"

Laura reached for a French fry, annoyed that Dylan's call had spoiled their celebratory mood. "I think he's a little jealous that I'm out with you. He shouldn't be."

"Of course not. I'm sorry if this causes any trouble for you." He looked uncomfortable and Laura spoke quickly to reassure him.

"Don't be ridiculous. I don't need his permission to go out with my friends."

Cole finished his last sip of beer and set his empty mug down. "I was going to suggest another drink, but maybe that's not such a good idea now."

"Probably not," Laura agreed as she reached for her glass which was almost empty. "He said he's waiting at home for me."

Cole insisted on picking up the check when the waitress brought it over and Laura finally agreed on the condition that she could return the favor.

"When are you heading back to Charleston?" she asked as they walked out to their vehicles.

"Tomorrow. I have a meeting with Rick in the morning and then I'll be heading home after that."

"You'll like Rick," she said as she reached her car. "I guess I'll see you in a month or so, when you're back in town. Unless I get up to Charleston before then. I'm still hoping that I'll be able to get away for a few days."

Cole smiled. "Well, if you do, be sure to give me a call. I'd love to show you around."

"I definitely will." He gave her a quick hug goodbye, and she watched him walk away as she got into her car. She was glad that he'd called her and she was thrilled for him. She knew exactly how he felt and it was exciting to see someone else go through what she'd already experienced. She felt such a strong comfort level with Cole, like no one else, except maybe Tina. But she still couldn't remember much about their past, only that there was one. It was frustrating to know her memories were so close, yet she still couldn't grasp hold of them.

As Laura drove home, she was already dreading the conversation with Dylan. She hadn't liked his tone. He clearly had trust issues, and he'd grown more controlling lately, ever since he'd given her the engagement ring. When she pulled into the driveway, he was leaning against his car with his arms folded. Laura took a deep breath as she got out of her car. She was grateful that she hadn't gotten around to giving him a key to her apartment. He'd asked for one more than once and she'd agreed but hadn't done it yet.

"Nice to see you, finally," Dylan said as Laura walked over to him. He pulled her in for a hug and a quick kiss. He seemed calm enough and there was even a hint of a smile as he suggested that they go inside. Laura relaxed a little. Maybe he wasn't as mad as she'd thought he'd be.

But once they were inside with the door closed behind them, his smile faded.

"So, why were you out with Cole? What's going on?"

Laura saw the anger in his eyes and noticed a muscle in his jaw flicker. Dylan was furious.

"Nothing is going on. Cole and I are friends. He got some good news today and wanted to share it with someone. Someone who understood."

"And what kind of news would you understand?"

Laura smiled, hoping to diffuse the tension in the room. "He signed with Black duck studios today. They want him to make an album."

"Well, isn't that great for him?" Dylan looked less than

pleased with the news. "So, how did he know how to get in touch with you? Did you give him your number?"

Laura took a step back, not liking the look in Dylan's eyes. She said nothing as he looked around the room and then picked up an empty beer bottle sitting on the counter.

"Yes, I gave him my number and asked him to keep in touch. That's what friends do."

Laura jumped as Dylan smashed the beer bottle down hard against the counter sending pieces of broken glass everywhere. His face took on a red flush as he shouted, "We're engaged! You will not be giving your number to any other guys from now on."

Laura stared at him in horror. Another memory suddenly flooded in. She was about thirteen and her mother had been dating a new guy for a couple of months. He had a temper and he and her mother got into a fight about something stupid and he smashed his fist into the wall. It terrified Laura at the time and it made her mother so furious that she broke up with him immediately and told Laura that it was a good lesson to never put up with anything like that.

Laura slowly worked her engagement ring off her finger and set it on the counter.

Dylan's jaw dropped. "What are you doing?"

"What I probably should've done when you gave the ring to me. I'm not ready for this and after what I just saw, I'm done."

"So, it's true then. You're getting back with Cole?"

Laura laughed. He was ridiculous. "No, I'm not. One,

we're just friends and two, the last I knew, Cole was still married."

"You're overreacting. Put the ring back on Laura. We can work this out." Dylan's tone was different now, calmer and almost pleading.

Laura shook her head sadly. "No, Dylan. We can't. I'm sorry."

"So that's it then? You seriously want to break up?" Dylan was annoyed again and frustrated.

"I do." Laura picked up the ring and handed it to him. He grabbed it from her and stuffed it in his pocket and turned to leave.

"This isn't over Laura," he said as he opened the front door.

Laura breathed a sigh of relief as soon as the door shut behind him. She grabbed the dustpan and brush and quickly cleaned up the broken glass in the kitchen. As soon as it was taken care of she collapsed on her sofa and pulled a soft throw blanket around her. She was sad about what just happened with Dylan, but she also felt like a giant weight had been lifted off her shoulders. She knew that she'd made the right decision to end things with him.

CHAPTER 27

Cole met with Rick in the morning and as Laura had predicted, he liked him quite a bit. Rick went over the Black Duck contract and explained all the fine print. Cole also signed an agreement with Rick for him to be his manager. Once the paperwork was finalized, the two of them shook hands and Rick promised to keep in touch over the coming weeks.

Cole's mind raced during the long drive home to Charleston. As excited as he was about everything going on with Black Duck, he was dreading sitting down with Chelsea when he got home. He was still optimistic though that they could find a way to make it work somehow.

Because the reality was that he was going to be spending a lot of time in Nashville once they started recording. He needed to line up some kind of temporary housing for short-term rental, maybe.

He thought a lot about Laura too as he drove. It was

great to see her again. As he always had, he just liked being around her. And now she even shared his passion for music. He'd been so excited to share his news with her. He was still furious with his father and the years he had robbed them both of. He could tell that Laura didn't fully remember their time together. She'd mentioned wanting to drive to Charleston and look around. He hoped that she would. Maybe once she saw where she used to live, where she grew up, she'd get more of those memories back. He needed her to remember how things once were with the two of them. Even if they would never be that way again, he wanted her to remember.

And he had a bad feeling about Dylan. Laura had seemed stressed out when he called while they were at the Black Rose. Cole hadn't wanted to leave yet. The time with her had flown by. He enjoyed her company and wasn't in a hurry to get back to his empty hotel room. But he could tell she was anxious to get home, and that Dylan was waiting for her. He seemed like a controlling jerk. She deserved better than that.

By the time he pulled in the driveway, it was dark but Chelsea wasn't home yet. He'd left her message earlier when he got on the road, to let her know that he was on his way. So, he was a little surprised that she wasn't there.

It was almost midnight before he heard a car outside. He'd gone up to bed around eleven, and as usual, locked all the doors. After a few minutes of silence, he went downstairs. Chelsea was still outside fumbling to find her keys. He opened the door, and she stumbled inside.

"Where have you been?" He wasn't mad just curious.

Chelsea set her bag on the kitchen table so close to the edge that it almost fell off. "Went out with friends after work," she said as she slid off her coat and slung it over a chair.

"Was it a special occasion?" It was late to be out on a weeknight.

"Austin's birthday." She slurred her words a little.

"How did you get home?" He'd noticed when he opened the door to let her in that her car wasn't in the driveway.

"Austin dropped me off. I left my car at the office."

"Well at least you didn't drive." Chelsea rarely had more than a few drinks and when she did, she was smart enough not to drive.

"When did you get home?" Chelsea asked as she poured herself a big glass of water.

"A few hours ago. It's late. We should both get to bed get some sleep. We'll talk in the morning."

"Okay," she agreed sleepily.

As they walked upstairs Dylan asked, "How many of you went out tonight?"

"Just me and Austin," she said. But a second later she added "No that's not right, the whole office went out. Sorry, I'm just really tired."

"No problem. Good night, Chelsea."

COLE WAS up early the next day and had already eaten breakfast and poured himself a second cup of coffee by the time Chelsea made her way downstairs. With one look he could tell she was horribly hung over, and he sympathized.

"There's plenty of coffee left. I made a big pot."

She almost smiled as she looked his way. "Thanks. I think I'll start with a huge glass of ice water. I dreamed about it, the water. It's what got me out of bed."

"That bad, huh?"

She groaned. "I had vodka. I hardly ever drink vodka. This never happens when I have wine."

She downed the glass and then refilled it and poured herself a cup of coffee too before joining Cole at the kitchen table. She slowly stirred a little sugar into her cup and took a tentative sip.

"It always comes out better when you make it."

Cole laughed. "I think that's just the hangover talking, but thanks."

Chelsea pressed her hand against her forehead and then looked around until she saw her purse on the other side of the table. She pulled it over, fished a bottle of ibuprofen out of it and downed a couple. Then she leaned back in her chair and slowly sipped her coffee. Cole stayed silent and waited for her to start the discussion he knew was coming.

"So, tell me about Nashville. What happens now?" she asked.

"It went well, really well. I signed a contract with Black Duck Studios and with a manager, good guy that represents Laura too."

Chelsea's eyes narrowed. "Did you see Laura when you were there?"

He smiled. "I did. She was excited for me. She's sending me a few songs to consider for my first album."

"Is she still engaged?" Cole wasn't sure if there was a hint of jealousy in her voice or just annoyance at the whole music thing.

"Yes. To one of the guys in her band. I'm not crazy about him though. He's kind of a jerk."

"Well, that's too bad. Not really your problem though."

"No, I suppose not," he agreed.

"So, what's the plan then? When are you leaving and how long will you be gone?"

"We start recording in about a month. I'm not sure how long it will take. I figured I'd look into a short-term rental, month-to-month kind of thing. I can come back most weekends as long as I don't have a gig lined up."

"You'll be performing already in Nashville?" Chelsea sounded surprised

Cole nodded. "Not right away, but Rick is looking into possibilities for me to get out there and be seen. To strike while people still remember me from the show, to leverage that."

Chelsea got up and topped off her coffee and then his before sitting down again.

She sighed. "I'm happy for you, I really am. This just isn't how I pictured our marriage."

"I've always been upfront with you about the music."

"I know." Chelsea chewed her bottom lip for a moment and then spoke. "I have to admit, I never thought it would go anywhere. You went to law school. I thought you'd work with your dad or another important firm in Charleston and we'd have a nice life together."

"We still can. And for the record, I never wanted to work for my father."

"I know. I thought you'd come around on that. I just had a vision of how I thought things would be, you know?"

Cole looked at her closely and asked the question he'd been wondering. "Is there anything going on with you and that Austin guy you work with?"

Chelsea looked startled by the question at first, and then she laughed. "With Austin? Of course not. We're just good friends and we've been working together a lot lately."

Cole believed her. "Okay, good."

She smiled. "He's going to be quite the catch for some girl though. His family is even richer than yours and he's on the fast track politically. People are excited about the possibility of him running for and winning a congressional seat in the next election. He's very charismatic."

"That's great." Cole couldn't help but notice how her face lit up as she talked about Austin and his future. It was everything she'd dreamed of. He understood how his music and having to spend so much time in Nashville must be a disappointment to her in comparison. Even though he'd been up front with her, it wasn't really what she thought she'd signed up for.

"I need to just see where this goes. It might not go anywhere, lots of first albums never do. I might be back here practicing law after all."

"That wouldn't be so bad, would it?" Chelsea brightened at the thought of it.

Cole said nothing. Coming back to Charleston, studying for the bar and becoming a lawyer meant failing. And he wasn't ready to think about that just yet.

CHAPTER 28

The next week was hell for Laura. She didn't regret ending things with Dylan, but she hadn't considered how messy it was going to be since they still had to work together. They had several gigs booked and after each one, Dylan insisted on talking to her and pleading his case, trying to convince her to get back together with him. She finally had to talk to Rick to see if they could reschedule an upcoming gig to open a weeklong break in her schedule. She told Dylan she was going out of town and when she came back, if they were going to still work together he needed to respect that her decision was final, or she'd ask Rick to start looking for another band for her to sing with. He didn't like it, but he agreed and she could sense that it was finally beginning to sink in for him that it was really and truly over.

She enjoyed a few quiet days to herself and decided to make the drive to Charleston mid-week for a night or two. Tina stopped by the night before she left and they enjoyed some wine together on the balcony, like they used to when they were roommates.

"I think going to Charleston is a good idea. Are you nervous?" Tina asked.

"Yes. Terrified and excited at the same time. I feel like I'll get answers there. Hopefully the missing pieces of my memory, at least some of them, will come back."

"It's still crazy to think Cole's father did that to the two of you."

"I know. It worked though. He's the governor now."

"Some say he wants to make a run for the presidency. Has Cole mentioned that?"

Laura wasn't surprised. "No, he doesn't talk about his father much. They're not close."

"I don't blame him. I'm not sure I'd ever speak to my father if he did that."

"I think it is hard for him though. He doesn't have much family left. Just his father and his Aunt Helen."

"His Aunt Helen. That's still the strangest thing to me too. That we thought she was your Aunt Helen."

"I know. And even though she's not really my aunt, we were close, and I thought she was family."

"Are you still talking to her at all?" Tina was curious.

"A little. I was furious of course. But I also got to know her son, Harold and on some level, I get it. She needed money for him."

"On a happier note. I'm glad you dumped Dylan. I never did like him much."

Laura laughed. "I know you didn't."

"Are you okay with that though? No second thoughts?" Tina sounded concerned and Laura loved her for it.

"I'm still sad that it didn't work. But there were signs. I probably should have ended it months ago. It was easier not to, to just drift along, as my focus was really more on getting the music right. And he was part of that. I knew it might be messy if we broke up and it has been."

"Yeah, that must be tough for both of you, to still work together so closely. Will you need to find a new band?"

"I hope not. I told Dylan I would though if things didn't get better. I think, hope, he knows that there's no chance of us getting back together."

"So, you're off to Charleston. What will you do first?" Tina added a little more chardonnay to their almost empty glasses.

Laura smiled. "I booked a room at a cute little bed-and-breakfast right in the heart of downtown Charleston. I thought it would be fun to play tourist. And I told Cole I'd call him if I came to town. He said he'd show me around. I'm hoping if I see where I lived, and places I used to go, that it might help me to remember more."

"That's big. And what about Cole? He's married right?"

Laura knew what she was asking. "He is married."

Tina looked disappointed. "Too bad."

Laura grinned. "I know right? We're good friends though. I am glad that he's back in my life."

Tina lifted her glass. "To finding happy memories in Charleston!"

LAURA SET out the next day for Charleston. She called Cole along the way and they made plans to meet up for lunch downtown the next day. He said he was excited to show her around. She'd planned on the trip taking a little over eight hours, but there was an accident on the highway that slowed things down and it was dark by the time she reached the bed-and-breakfast. She was exhausted by the day of driving and eager to take a long hot shower.

The bed-and-breakfast was lovely and Laura felt like she was stepping back in time as she walked into the stately old home that dated back to the mid 1800's. An older woman with a perfect blonde bob and a friendly smile greeted her at the front desk.

"Welcome, I'm Rose Taylor. Are you checking in with us?"

"Yes. Laura Scott, for two nights."

Rose looked in her reservation book and then handed her a key. "You're in the yellow room, one of our nicest. It gets a lot of sun. Oh, and I just need your credit card again dear. You won't be charged until you check out of course."

A few minutes later, Laura was settled in her room. It was pretty and cozy too, with a gas fireplace, a four-poster bed and a bathroom that made her sigh with happiness when she saw the oversized claw-foot tub. She couldn't wait to soak in it. After a long, hot bath, she felt much better. Once her hair was dried, she set out for a walk to find something to eat.

There was a cute little market a few doors down from

the hotel that had sandwiches and several homemade soups. That sounded perfect to Laura. She ordered a bowl of creamy crab soup and a hot roll to go and brought it back to her room. Charleston was famous for she-crab soup and it was delicious. By the time she finished eating, her eyes were growing heavy again, and she decided to put on her pajamas and crawl into bed. She needed a good night's sleep, as tomorrow was going to be a big day.

Just as she reached to turn out the light, her cell phone dinged, and she saw that it was another text message from Dylan. He'd been leaving her messages wanting to get together and talk and she knew there was no point to it. She'd meant it when she said she was done. She frowned though as she read his latest text message. "If you don't reply, you will be sorry." Laura responded by turning off her cellphone and flipping the switch on her bedside lamp.

CHAPTER 29

L aura woke early, around six when the sun steamed through the windows. She'd forgotten to pull the heavy curtains shut before she went to bed. She didn't mind though. She liked to get up early and was both excited and nervous to explore the city. She dressed and made her way downstairs for breakfast, which was included. There was a table with all kinds of pastries, fresh cut fruit, several quiches, and an assortment of breads and bagels. She helped herself to a cup of black coffee, a bowl of fruit and a bagel with butter. She had the room to herself until she was almost done eating and a lovely older couple, Mavis and Tom Ellis, joined her and said they were from Boston.

"It's our first time here. Have you been to Charleston before?" Mavis asked as she buttered a thick slice of pecan and raisin toast.

"I lived here when I was young, but I haven't been

back in many years. It feels new to me too," Laura admitted.

"How fun for you to see where you grew up! If we run into each other at breakfast tomorrow, you'll have to tell us all about it."

Laura promised to do so and then left them to enjoy their breakfast. A thought had come to her as she chatted with the older couple and saw how they seemed to adore each other and were so excited to go on a historic tour they had booked. They seemed to be the best of friends and Laura knew that's what she wanted in a partner too. Someone she could relax and have fun with and adore. She could feel a song building and was anxious to get back to her room and get the words down that matched the images and sounds in her mind.

The next few hours flew as the song came together quickly. When she had it where she wanted it to be, she recorded it on her cellphone, then hit play. As she listened, Laura felt the goosebumps that indicated she'd hit onto something really good. Maybe she'd play it for Cole when she saw him and see what he thought.

At a few minutes to noon, Laura headed downstairs to the lobby to wait for Cole. He was already there and smiled when he saw her.

"I hope I didn't keep you waiting?"

"Not at all. I just got here a few minutes ago. Traffic was lighter than I expected." He glanced around the lobby at the colorful arrangements of flowers scattered throughout the room. The sunlight streaming through the windows warmed the room and highlighted the older furniture that had been lovingly restored. It was an elegant and cozy setting. "Pretty place."

"It is," Laura agreed. "I just wrote a song this morning that I kind of like. I'd love to get your opinion on it later. I taped it on my cellphone."

"I'd love to hear it. I'd be honored to be the first one to listen."

"I'd love to know what you think of it and you must promise to be completely honest. I want real feedback."

Cole grinned. "I promise. So, how do you feel about grabbing some sandwiches and having a picnic lunch? There's a park we used to go to, right near downtown, and maybe we can get an ice-cream after, if we feel like it."

"That sounds perfect. There's a place a few doors down that has sandwiches."

"Lead the way."

———

TWENTY MINUTES LATER, they reached the park and Laura followed Cole to a large tree that had a bench beside it. Laura was happily surprised that it looked familiar and she could feel that she'd been there before. The sun was shining and there was no wind, so it was nice and warm as they sat eating their turkey sandwiches. Cole pointed out various landmarks as they ate, a bookstore on the corner that Laura spend many hours in, the pizza shop they used to buy slices at and the ice cream store.

"I wonder if they have almond fudge chip?" Laura asked.

Cole laughed. "They do. That was always your favorite."

"Really? That's a good sign then. And this all looks vaguely familiar to me, kind of a déjà vu feeling."

"Do you remember this?" Cole pointed to a rough carving on the tree next to them. A heart with their initials inside."

"You did that?"

"I did. We were crazy about each other then."

Laura felt a rush of emotion and sadness for what they'd both lost. It wasn't hard to imagine being in love with Cole. She felt so comfortable with him and her heart ached for their teen-aged selves.

"I wish I could remember more. It feels like it's starting to come back though, slowly."

Cole gathered up their empty sandwich wraps and tossed them in the trash can behind their bench. "So, now that we've eaten, let's hear your song, and then if you have room, we can go get that ice cream."

Laura pulled her cell phone out of her purse and found the recording. She suddenly felt shy as she hit play. She always did when anyone heard a song of hers for the first time. It was hard to know what people would like and sometimes she knew she was too close to it to be objective. As the song played, she relaxed. It still sounded pretty good. And not for the first time, she felt a wave of sadness that Cole was married. If fate had brought them back together, it seemed like a cruel twist for both of them to be with other people—though, she was single now and had no plans to rush into a relationship with anyone anytime soon.

The sound of clapping snapped Laura out of her daydreaming. Cole was holding his hand up to high five her and he looked excited. She slapped her hand against his as he began speaking.

"That was phenomenal. I think maybe your best song yet. It's going to pull on people's heartstrings."

"Thank you! I'm so glad you liked it. Is there anything you'd want to change?" Laura often got her best tweaks to a song after people made suggestions and once she implemented them, it made the song even better.

Cole thought about it for a moment. "It's pretty perfect, but there was one thing I thought of. What if you went a little softer at the midpoint and then let it build a little more at the end? Might be a more powerful finish."

Laura knew he was right. She could hear the adjustment in her mind and knew it was the right finishing touch.

"I'll do that, thanks."

"So, are you ready for that ice cream?"

THEY GOT their ice cream cones, almond fudge chip for her and pistachio for him, and then strolled along the busy street as they ate them, stopping now and then to peek in the windows of different shops. They went back to Cole's truck after that and spent the rest of the afternoon sightseeing.

He took her all over town to all the places they used to go. Some places felt more familiar than others. When they went to Folly Beach to the spot where they used to always go, Laura felt the same bittersweetness that she'd felt at the tree. She could feel that they spent a lot of time at that beach and it was important to them. It was a beautiful place and she couldn't resist walking barefoot on the sand and dipping her toes in the water.

When they left the beach, Cole said the last stops would be the high school they attended and the trailer park where she used to live with her mother. They drove by the high school first and Laura was surprised by the rush of memories that swept over her as she looked at the familiar school. She'd been happy there. It was confusing to have so many memories filling her up at once. It made her head ache, and she pressed one hand against her temple.

"Are you okay?" Cole sounded concerned.

She smiled and tried not to show how shaken she was. "I'm fine. It just took me by surprise because it looked so familiar. That hasn't really happened yet."

"Are you sure you want to go to your mother's place today? We can put it off if you want."

"No, I'm sure. I want to go there. I feel like I need to."

Cole nodded. "Okay then. It's right around the corner. We'll be there in a few minutes."

Laura held her breath as Cole turned onto Sutton Street. As soon as she saw the street sign, she recognized it. Cole pulled into the trailer park and slowed down as he reached number eighteen. There a cheerful older woman sitting on the patio drinking a cup of coffee while a skinny orange cat walked in figure eights around her feet.

She smiled and looked at them curiously when they got out of the truck.

"Can I help you? Are you looking for someone that lives in the park?" she asked.

"No, we're just passing through," Cole said.

"I used to live here, in your unit. Years ago," Laura told her.

The woman looked delighted to hear it. "You did? How marvelous. Would you like a look around? I've redecorated in my style, but I haven't really changed anything. It was in very good condition. I'm Betty, by the way."

"I'm Laura and this is Cole. I'd love a look around, if it's not too much trouble."

"No trouble at all. I welcome the company. It's quiet around here during the day. Come on in."

Laura and Cole followed her inside and as she showed them around, chattering all the while, Laura felt a little fuzzy as if she was in a dream walking around. She remembered living here, and when Laura stepped into her old bedroom, she felt light-headed as a deluge of memories crashed down on her. All kinds of images and feelings all at once; it was overwhelming. She swayed and Cole put his hand on her arm to steady her.

"Are you okay?" he whispered.

She nodded, but when Cole took her hand to lead her out of the room, she gripped onto it tightly. When they went into Betty's bedroom, her mother's old room, Laura's eyes welled up and the sadness was almost more than she could bear. She fought back the tears and tried to gather herself together. She didn't want to fall apart in front of

Betty or Cole. She could do that later when she was alone in her room and could figure out how she was going to deal with everything that she remembered. Because now, she remembered it all. She remembered being in love with Cole. She glanced at his sweet concerned face and wanted to burrow herself in his arms, to hold tight and never let go. But she knew that wasn't possible.

CHAPTER 30

Cole's phone dinged as he and Laura said goodbye to Betty and climbed into his truck. He glanced at the text message, which was from Chelsea.

"Don't wait for me for dinner. Working late tonight. Not sure what time I'll be home."

It was the second time that week she'd worked late. As he and Laura pulled out of the trailer park, a thought came to him since he was on his own now for the evening.

"That was Chelsea. She's working late tonight and I'm not much of a cook. Want to join me for dinner?" He wasn't ready to drop Laura off yet and he was a little worried about her.

"I'd love that. I was probably just going to have soup again and hibernate in my room. Dinner with you sounds much better." She was smiling again and seemed back to normal, so maybe he'd imagined that she was sad or upset before. Laura always had been on the reserved side. She kept things to herself and wasn't always easy to read.

"Great! You like barbecue right?"

"Love it. Nashville has the best."

Cole grinned. "Well, you haven't had Smoky Pete's yet. It's kind of a dive, an out of the way place, but it's the best I've ever had. The margaritas are good too."

"That sounds wonderful. I'm sure I'll love it."

Twenty minutes later, they arrived at Smoky Pete's and Laura laughed as she followed Cole down into the basement of a brick building in what looked like a sketchy part of town.

"I told you it was a dive," Cole said before a hostess came over to seat them and handed them menus. When the waitress came, they both ordered margaritas which were delivered a few minutes later in salt-rimmed mason jars. She also set down a bowl of hot roasted peanuts to snack on.

"I think it's charming," Laura said as she looked around the room. Cole followed her gaze, seeing the restaurant through her eyes. It had cement floors with crushed peanut shells littered here and there. Small windows with faded black shutters let in a hint of light, but otherwise the room was dark and dimly lit except for colored lights strung along the walls and wrapped around tall beams. Booths with brown faux leather seats lined the walls and there were a few cocktail tables in the middle. There was usually live music most nights. Later in the evening, the restaurant turned into more of a bar and the tables would be pushed to one side to make room for dancing.

From where they sat they could see the open kitchen where workers were slicing meat and cooking their meals.

It was a good place to go if you didn't want to be bothered. When he and Chelsea were first dating they used to go often and hide out in a booth for hours, laughing and drinking margaritas, happy in their own little world. They hadn't been there in a long time, almost a year now.

"So, what's good here? What should I get?" Laura asked as she reached for a peanut and cracked open the shell.

"Everything's good. I usually get either the pulled pork or the brisket with mac and cheese on the side."

When their waitress came over, Cole ordered the brisket and Laura got the pulled pork. Their food came out quickly, and they chatted easily as they ate. But Laura didn't say anything about how she was feeling or what if anything she'd remembered that day. Cole was pretty sure she remembered something because she seemed not quite herself when they were at the trailer and even before when they drove by the high school she looked miles away. His mind went back to her new song, which spoke to him. It was how he'd always viewed their relationship, when they were together. She said it was inspired by the older couple she'd met at breakfast, but he couldn't help wondering if somewhere deep inside her subconscious she was starting to remember and it was coming out in her music.

"Penny for your thoughts? You look a million miles away." Laura smiled at him as she reached for a French fry and dunked it in the tangy barbeque sauce.

He laughed. "They're not worth that much. Just enjoying the food. What do you think of it?"

"It's as good as you said. I can see why you like it here."

"Are you doing any more sight-seeing tomorrow? I can suggest a few places."

"No, I have to head back early tomorrow. We actually have a gig tomorrow night. I was hoping to move the date, but it didn't work out."

Cole was disappointed that she was leaving so soon and she didn't look happy about it either.

"That's going to be a long day. What time is your gig?"

"We're not going on until nine. If I get an early start, I should be fine."

"I'll be heading back myself in a few weeks. I still need to line up a place to stay. Let me know if you hear of any short-term rentals?"

"I will. How is Chelsea feeling about everything? Do you think she'll come visit you in Nashville?"

Cole wasn't sure if Chelsea had ever actually been to Nashville, but he knew she had no desire to go there anytime soon—even if he was there.

"No, I don't think so. She's busy with work."

"Maybe for a long weekend even?" Laura sounded hopeful and Cole guessed that she couldn't imagine not wanting to see her husband on the weekend. At first, it had bothered him that she didn't seem to care about seeing him. Now he just shrugged it off to Chelsea being Chelsea.

"It's not really her thing, the whole music scene. She tolerates it, barely."

"I'm sorry. She doesn't know what she's missing!" Cole saw the sympathy in her eyes and appreciated it. Their waitress came by to clear their plates and they decided to have another round of margaritas for dessert.

"How's Dylan? I wasn't sure if he might come to Charleston with you." He was surprised actually that Dylan had let Laura go without him.

Laura took a slow sip of her drink as a cloud darkened her eyes.

"We broke up actually. I gave him his ring back. It was the night I saw you at the pub."

Cole was shocked and glanced at her ring finger, which was bare. He hadn't even noticed it before.

"I'm sorry to hear it. I hope I didn't make things difficult for you?" It was obvious that Dylan didn't like him.

"No, not at all. This was a long time coming. I should never have accepted his proposal. It was too soon and ultimately, it just became apparent that he wasn't the one for me. He was too controlling, too jealous. It was exhausting."

Cole nodded. "Well, I'm glad you ended it before things got too ugly."

Laura smiled and looked relieved. "I am too. I'm content to be very single for a while."

"Well, cheers to that." Cole tapped his glass against hers. A few minutes later, two guys in the corner of the room started playing some blues music. They were really good, and they enjoyed listening to a few songs while they finished their drinks. Cole paid the check and saw that there was a line of people waiting for tables. The restaurant and bar area were both packed.

As they walked out, he saw a familiar face out of the corner of his eye and took a step back for a better look. Laura didn't see him stop and kept walking while Cole stood for a moment, watching his wife sitting in a booth, drinking a glass of wine and laughing at something her co-worker, Austin was saying. It was just the two of them.

Cole pulled his phone out and checked it. There was no new message from Chelsea. Just the earlier one about working late. He started to take a step in their direction to say hello. Maybe they'd just finished earlier than expected and went for a bite to eat. But, then he saw Chelsea rest her hand on Austin's wrist and something about their body language made him hesitate. He decided to wait until later and see if she mentioned it herself.

———

LAURA STEPPED outside and was surprised that Cole wasn't right behind her. She stepped to the side of the door and waited for him to come out. A few minutes later, he joined her and looked liked he'd seen a ghost.

"What's wrong?" she asked.

He paused for a moment and it seemed like he was about to tell her, but instead, he ran a hand distractedly through his hair as he led the way to his truck.

"Nothing. Sorry I kept you waiting. I thought I saw someone I knew, but I was wrong."

Laura still sensed that something was on his mind as he was quieter than he'd been all day during the drive back to her bed-and-breakfast. When they reached it, he parked and walked her to the door.

"Thank you so much for showing me around. It was a wonderful day, and it helped, so much!" Laura hugged Cole hard and after a moment, he hugged her back and she could feel his energy, his need to be comforted. She didn't want the hug to end, but when it did, she was happy to see that he looked himself again.

"It was a great day. I'm glad it was helpful too," Cole said. There was something so warm and caring in his eyes that it touched her and she felt a sudden rush of sadness. She couldn't help but wonder, if Chelsea wasn't in the picture, if they might have found their way back to each other. She felt a bit guilty for the thought though because he was very much married. She and Cole could be friends, good friends even, but nothing more.

"Good night, Cole. See you soon in Nashville."

CHAPTER 31

Cole got home a little before eight. His original plan was to confront Chelsea as soon as she got home, but the more he thought about it, he decided to wait. He thought it would be a conversation best had in the sober sunlight of morning. Plus, he had no idea what time she would even get home. He changed into an old t-shirt and sweats and headed out for a run. He was too wide awake to just sit around waiting for her.

He ran for a good six or seven miles, his mind racing the whole time. He thought about Chelsea and he knew in his gut that something was going on with that Austin guy. Or if it wasn't yet, it looked like both of them wanted it. What surprised Cole the most was that he wasn't as upset by the idea as he'd thought he would be. He was more irritated than upset and oddly enough, he wasn't all that jealous. He wondered if it would be different if he'd been with Laura and saw her having an intimate dinner with someone other than him, and he realized when he looked down and saw his hands clenched into a fist that it would be.

He ran until he was exhausted and his mind finally calmed. After a quick shower, he settled in to watch the news and around eleven, he made his way up to bed. He fell asleep around midnight but slept lightly and woke when Chelsea finally climbed into bed. A glance at the alarm clock glowing on the nightstand showed that it was almost two am.

CHELSEA WAS STILL ASLEEP when Cole woke the next morning and went downstairs. He made a pot of coffee and scrambled a few eggs while he waited for her. About an hour later, she came down, showered and dressed for work. She looked ready to rush out the door.

"Coffee?" he offered as he topped off his own mug.

"Can't today, running late. I'll see you later."

"Not just yet. Sit down."

She looked irritated but also startled at the tone of his voice and joined him at the kitchen table. She sat on the edge of her seat, poised to run as soon as they were done.

"What is it?"

"Where were you last night?" Cole asked calmly. He took a sip of coffee as he watched her reaction. She didn't give him one, not right away.

"I told you where I was, working late." The irritation at being questioned was evident.

"It was nearly two before you got home. You were at the office the entire time?"

Something flashed across her face. Surprise perhaps that he'd been aware of what time she got in.

"Yes, of course. We were all there trying to meet a deadline. It was intense."

"I'm sure it was. What did you do about dinner?"

She was taken aback by that. "Dinner? We got takeout as usual." She was flat-out lying to his face now.

"Are you sure about that?" he asked quietly and could immediately see her wheels turn. Chelsea wasn't stupid.

"This week has been a blur. I got my nights mixed up. You're right, we didn't get takeout last night. We ran out for a quick bite to eat. We went to that place you and I used to go to."

Cole nodded. "Yeah, I saw you there actually, as I was leaving. You and Austin looked pretty deep in conversation so I didn't want to interrupt."

A range of emotions flashed across Chelsea's face—surprise, guilt, nervousness and curiosity.

"Who were you there with? I didn't see you."

"Laura was in town. I showed her around and since you said you weren't going to be home for dinner, she was kind enough to keep me company."

"Laura Scott? Your ex-girlfriend? And you're giving me grief about having dinner with a co-worker?"

"Laura and I are friends. Nothing more." Cole paused before adding, "I got a very different vibe when I saw you with Austin."

Chelsea's cheeks turned pink. "That's ridiculous!"

"Is it? You've been distant lately. Ever since I first went to Nashville."

"And now you're going back to Nashville for God knows how long! I just didn't expect it to be like this."

"Like what?"

"I thought you'd give up on the music thing and we'd have a nice life here," Chelsea said dramatically. "Austin and I are just friends. There's nothing going on. But I do enjoy his company and he's going places here in Charleston and maybe even on the national political scene someday. It's exciting."

"I'm sure it is. I don't really know what to say to that. What do you want to do?"

"What do you mean do?"

Cole sighed. "You're obviously not happy with me. With where I'm going. Do you want a divorce?"

She looked shocked. "Of course not! That's ridiculous. Every marriage goes through ups and downs. We'll get through this. Go do your Nashville thing and get it out of your system. You'll be back full-time after that right? In a month or two?"

"I don't really know. It depends how things go. I'll be back after that, but I'll be back and forth to Nashville as needed."

"Well, we'll cross that bridge when we get there. So, are we good? I'm going to be really late if I don't go now."

"Go ahead and go."

"I'll be home early. We'll have a quiet night in." Chelsea smiled big and then bolted for the door.

And Cole was left feeling more confused than ever. He

wanted to believe her, but he knew what he'd seen and sensed at the restaurant. Maybe it was completely innocent? A quiet night in might be good for both of them.

But Chelsea called later that afternoon to say that she wouldn't be home early after all.

"The client didn't love our proposal. We have to start over from scratch and present something new tomorrow. I'm afraid it's going to be another late night."

Cole hung up the phone and sighed. He felt the urge for another long run as the long night stretched ahead of him. Maybe he'd work on songwriting for a while too. An idea had come to him as he'd drifted off to sleep the night before, something about a marriage in trouble and the lies and affair that ended it. He wasn't sure how it would go but he sensed that it would have a bittersweet ending. He was also strangely excited to get it down. He had a feeling that he was onto something good.

CHAPTER 32

Laura made it back to Nashville with just about enough time to shower and change before heading out to meet the rest of the band. They were playing at one of the bigger clubs in the city and one Laura had only been to once before but as a customer. There was a good crowd already there when she arrived. The guys were there getting set up on stage and she joined them. Dylan nodded when he saw her.

"We can go on in ten if you're ready?"

"I'm as ready as I'll ever be."

They played two sets, with a short break in between. Everything went smoothly, and the crowd was great. Laura closed the night singing her new song, the one she'd written in Charleston and since the other guys didn't know it yet, it was just her and her guitar. And the crowd loved it.

"That new song was amazing. You wrote that?" Dylan asked when they were walking off the stage. Laura was relieved that he was being friendly and normal. The tenseness that had been there seemed to be gone.

"Yes, just yesterday."

"It went over really well. I think you may have another hit on your hands."

"Thank you."

"Want to grab a quick drink? I'd love to catch up."

Laura hesitated, but then she figured why not? The other guys in the band would probably be joining them and they'd all have a drink together.

"Sure, I could stay for a quick one."

They all walked to the bar, but after Dylan handed her a beer, he led her to a quiet table in the corner and it was just the two of them.

"Oh, I thought we'd be joining the others?" Laura was beginning to regret her decision to stay.

"We can see them any time. I really wanted to talk to you. I've missed you."

Laura didn't know what to say to that. She hadn't missed Dylan at all. She stayed quiet, trying to think of what to say. But Dylan kept talking.

"So, now that we've had some time apart, I'm hoping we can give this another shot? I really think we could be great together. I love you, Laura." He put his hand on hers, and Laura knew he was trying to show his feelings but the only thing she felt was trapped. She pulled her hand away and crossed her arms in front of her.

"I'm sorry, Dylan. I think you're great. I really do. But I haven't changed my mind."

His expression instantly changed from calm to stormy.

He was holding his beer and set it down so hard on the table that people around them turned at the sound. But he didn't seem to notice.

"So, what then? Are you with him now? That guy you met at the pub?" A muscle flickered in his jaw and Laura could see the whites of his knuckles, he was gripping his bottle of beer so hard.

Laura shook her head. Dylan clearly couldn't accept the fact that she just didn't want to be with him. He assumed there had to be another man involved.

"No. I've told you before. Cole is married. I'm sorry Dylan. Really sorry that it didn't work out with us. But I'm not going to change my mind." She took a sip of her beer, which was still more than half full and set the bottle down, then stood up. "I'm going home now. Have a good night."

Dylan said nothing as Laura quickly walked away. She couldn't wait to get home. A half hour later, she was curled up on her sofa, watching a sitcom and trying not to think about anything. She did feel bad about Dylan, but she was sure of her feelings that it would never work with him.

And her thoughts kept going back to Cole. She'd been floored when her memories came flooding back when they were together. It was overwhelming, and she'd tried not to show shaken she was. She hadn't felt right about telling Cole that she remembered everything, especially how in love they were. Not now that he was happily married.

The drive home from Charleston had been a painful one as her many memories fought for her attention. She alternated from feeling the joy she'd experienced with Cole to the devastating sadness when she thought about her mother and then all the years that Cole's father had stolen from them.

And now she understood why she hadn't fallen seriously in love with anyone since. She'd always held back and been hesitant to get too serious. How could she? Cole had set a very high bar, and it was confusing now that she had her memories back because she felt that love again. And she knew it was wrong, and that she needed to move on. But she also knew that wasn't going to be easy, and it wasn't going to happen any time soon.

ole decided to head back to Nashville a week early to give himself time to find a place and settle in. And also because he didn't want to stay in Charleston another day. It was becoming increasingly clear that his marriage was over. Nothing changed with Chelsea. They hadn't slept together in weeks. She was always too tired, and he was often in bed by the time she got home. She never worked these kinds of hours when she started at the firm. It seemed to start around the time she first mentioned her new co-worker, Austin. And he was tired of hearing about him.

Chelsea talked about him non-stop, about what they were working on and how impressive Austin was. Cole wasn't impressed. He was sick of it. He wanted a divorce, but he decided that he was going to go to Nashville first, keep his focus on putting together the best record he was capable of and then he'd come home and deal with Chelsea.

As soon as he drove into Nashville, he felt his mood lift. It already felt like coming home to him. He booked a room at the same hotel he'd stayed at before and checked his calendar for the next day. He'd gone online before he left Charleston, made some calls and had three different rentals lined up to look at the next day. Hopefully one of them would work and he'd be able to settle in by the end of the week.

His stomach rumbled, and he pulled out his cellphone to check the time. It was a quarter past six. While he was debating what to do for dinner, his phone rang and he smiled when he saw that it was Laura.

"You must be psychic. I just got into town about a half hour ago. How are you?"

"You're here already? I didn't think you were coming for another week?" She sounded surprised.

"I decided to come early. Long story. What's up?" Cole picked up something in her voice that he couldn't place. Concern maybe? Laura never called him just to say hello.

"So you've been driving all day and probably haven't seen the news?"

"Haven't seen a thing. What have I missed?"

"It's awful, Cole. It's all over the news. What your father did. Me, you. They're insinuating that we're together and that you're cheating on your wife. My phone has been ringing off the hook and I haven't commented yet. I wanted to talk to you first."

Cole's immediate reaction was to laugh. "That's rich

that they think I'm cheating." But then he changed his tone because she was obviously upset. "I'm sorry this is happening. How did they find out?"

"I don't know. I've been wondering about it all day. Not many people know and the ones who do would never say anything. Except maybe Dylan. He wasn't happy with me the other night."

"I thought you ended things with him?" Cole didn't like to think of the two of them back together.

"I did. But we still work together, which is a little awkward. But I thought it seemed like he was doing okay with it. So I agreed to have a drink with everyone after our set a few weeks ago. But Dylan wanted to talk to me alone and wanted to get back together. He wasn't happy when I told him it was never going to happen. It's been very tense ever since having to work with him."

"Do you really think it was him? If it was, you should kick him out of the band." Cole was furious on her behalf.

"I really don't know. If it was him, then I agree. But it's not that simple. The band is his. I'd need to find a new one to sing with. So, it's just a mess. And reporters are hounding me."

"Can you duck out? We can meet somewhere to hash this out. I was just thinking about where to get some food, I'm starving."

"I haven't eaten yet either. Let's go to that pub we went to before. I can meet you there in about twenty minutes if I leave now," Laura said.

THE PUB WAS ONLY ABOUT ten minutes from where Cole was staying so he jumped in the shower to wash off the long drive first. His hair was still a little damp when he arrived at the pub. Laura was just settling onto a bar stool when he walked in. She smiled when she saw him and he walked over to her and gave her a hug before sitting on the empty stool next to her.

"It's so good to see you." Laura smiled and for a moment Cole remembered when she used to smile at him like that all the time. It warmed his heart and for the first time in weeks he began to relax. The situation with Chelsea had been stressful to say the least.

"It's always great to see you." Cole grinned as the bartender came over to take their drink order. They both ordered draft beers and after a quick look at the menu, Laura got a bar pizza and Cole ordered a burger with fries. While they waited for their food, Laura filled him in even more.

"It's all over the internet now, different news media, Facebook. As angry as I am at your father, I wanted to talk to you first before I answer any questions from the media."

"Thank you, but I don't care what you say about my father. There's no reason to protect him. He did what he did."

"I know that. It's you I care about. I don't want this to reflect badly on you in any way as you work on getting your first album out."

Cole hadn't considered that. "I don't see how it can be any worse than what they're already saying, about me cheating. But seriously, say whatever you like. Tell the truth."

Laura nodded. "Okay. One of the things they asked me was if I'm going to press charges. I never thought about that. But I don't think that I want to. It's not just your father that would be hurt."

"Aunt Helen," Cole said.

"I know she was wrong to go along with your father, but I don't think I could possibly send her to jail. Which means I won't press charges. I don't want to dredge it all up again. I just want it to go away, and to move on. If that makes sense?"

"It makes perfect sense," Cole agreed as the bartender set their meals in front of them.

"I'm going to ruin your father's plans," Laura said as she picked up a slice of pizza.

"For being president one day? Probably. Not your fault though. I don't see any way to really avoid it unless you were to lie about what happened. Which of course you can't do."

"No. I won't lie for him. We'll just see what happens I guess. I'll say as little as possible. And of course I'll deny that there's anything going on between us if asked."

Cole laughed. "Thanks. It does seem bizarre, doesn't it? The way these rumors start?"

"They'd love for it to be true...think about it. Young lovers torn apart and then reunited years later. Even better if I were to tear a marriage apart. Makes for a good story I guess."

"The media are like vultures," Cole agreed.

"The ironic thing is that I thought that Chelsea might actually be cheating on me."

Laura looked shocked. "I thought you were happy?"

Cole sighed. "We were once. But it's been different ever since we got married to be honest and especially since I came to Nashville. She never liked me doing music. Chelsea is all about image and she was excited for me to pass the bar and work for my father. That fit her vision of our marriage."

"But she must have always known you loved music?" Laura looked so confused.

"Oh, she did, but she never thought of it as more than a hobby. She didn't think it would go anywhere, and I'd get it out of my system."

"Sounds like she doesn't know you very well," Laura said softly. Something about her tone made Cole look at her more closely. As usual, whenever he saw her, it was so comfortable, almost as if no time had passed. He always felt better spending time with her.

"Chelsea's great, but it was never the same as it was with us. It was the next step and at the time I thought maybe it was good enough. But I was wrong."

Laura rested her hand lightly on his and gave it a reassuring squeeze. "Well, she's crazy then. You're a catch!"

Cole tried not to think about the fact that even now, years later, the slightest touch of Laura's skin gave his senses a jolt. For him, the attraction was still there, as strong as ever.

"Thanks. You always did know what to say."

They finished eating and ordered another round of

beers. Laura was so easy to talk to and they chatted easily about everything and nothing. He was almost done with his beer when he remembered he hadn't told her about the new song he'd written.

"I'd love to get your opinion on a song I wrote, if you have time sometime soon?"

"You wrote something! When can I hear it?" Laura sounded so excited that it made Cole laugh.

"Anytime. You tell me. My schedule is pretty open for the next week."

"What about now? After we finish here? I can stop by your place on the way home."

"Oh, sure. That would be great. Are you sure?"

"Yes, I'm sure. Let's go."

CHAPTER 34

C ole's cell phone rang as he was pulling out of the restaurant parking lot. It was Chelsea.

"I assume you've seen the news?" she asked.

"I heard, yeah. It's not true you know, what they're suggesting about me and Laura."

"I know. I know you. But still, it's ugly and frankly Cole, I don't want to be associated with it. I know it won't look good for you, but I think it's probably best for both of us if we get divorced. This hasn't been working for a while now."

"No, it hasn't," Cole agreed.

"I can go see someone this week and file papers if you're okay with it?"

"That's fine. I'll call an attorney too." A thought occurred to him.

"Was this your idea, or Austin's?"

Chelsea was quiet for a minute. "It was his actually.

But I agreed. We want to be together Cole, but I told him I wouldn't cheat on you, on anyone."

"Well, thanks for that. I guess." Cole pulled into his hotel driveway and parked. Laura pulled up next to him and got out of her car.

"So, you're sure you're alright with this? I can contact my attorney tomorrow?" She sounded anxious, excited and a little sad at the same time.

"I'm all right with it, Chelsea. We both deserve to be happy." Truth be told, she'd made it easier for him. Now he wouldn't be dreading having the conversation when he got home.

"Bye, Cole."

LAURA WAS WAITING for him when he got out of his truck and walked over to her.

"What's wrong?" She looked concerned and Cole was amazed that she could still sense his moods so well.

"Chelsea just called. She saw the news reports, and she asked me for a divorce. She beat me to it. I was going to ask her when I went home next. I just didn't want to deal with it until after I was done with the recording."

"I'm so sorry! But, if you were going to ask her, maybe it's a good thing?" Laura looked uncertain and worried for him.

He smiled to reassure her. "It just took me by surprise. It's sad, but good at the same time, if that makes sense."

She nodded. "It does. It's hard to end a relationship but

with Dylan, there was a little sadness but mostly relief and the certainty that I'd made the right decision."

"Yeah, I think that's how I'll feel too, once it sinks in." He unlocked the door to his room and held it open for Laura to step inside. The hotel room was basic, with two queen beds a small sitting area and bathroom. He picked up his guitar and sat on the side of one of the beds while Laura sat in one of the chairs.

He took a deep breath. "Okay, are you ready? Given what I'm accused of, it's a little ironic, but here we go." He started strumming and then sang the song straight through, glancing Laura's way now and then. Each time she was listening intently and smiled when she caught his eye. When the song ended, she stood and clapped slowly.

"That was incredible. You have to put it on the album. It may be your first hit. I got goosebumps. See!" She pulled her thin cotton sleeve up to show him her upper arm and it did have tiny raised bumps all over it. He grinned at the compliment.

"I hoped you'd like it. It felt good. Like I was in the zone when it came out. If that makes any sense?"

Laura nodded. "Perfect sense. Time disappears when I get locked into the zone. It's a beautiful thing."

"Is there anything you think I should change?" He respected her opinion.

"Well, I was thinking that maybe in that second verse, if you go a little lower and hold the note longer, it might be more dramatic when you hit that high note at the end. Kind of build up to it."

Cole sang the verse again and tried it the way Laura

suggested. "Better?" he asked when he finished.

"That's perfect. Really. Do it just like that. Everyone will love it."

"You're amazing. Thank you."

Laura stood. "I should probably go. What are you up to tomorrow? You're not going into the studio yet?"

"No, no until next week. I have a few places lined up to see tomorrow."

"Why don't you come for dinner tomorrow night? I don't have a gig and I'd love to cook you a home-cooked meal since you keep insisting on paying when we've gone out so far. Unless you're busy, of course."

Even if he did have plans, Cole would have rescheduled them to spend time with Laura.

"I would love to come for dinner."

"Then I'll see you at six. Good luck with the rentals tomorrow."

Cole walked Laura to her car and gave her a hug goodbye. It had been a great ending to an otherwise crappy day. He wasn't back in his hotel room for more than ten minutes when his phone rang again and he almost let it go to voice mail. It was his father and Cole figured it was easier to get the call over with than to dread calling him back.

"Hi Dad. What's up?"

"What do you think is up? You've seen the news? It's a disaster."

Cole was silent for a moment. "Dad, I don't know what you want me to say to that."

"Have you seen her?"

"I just had dinner with her."

This time his father was stunned into silence. "Is it true then?"

Cole laughed. "No, of course it's not true. You know me better than that."

"Good. Didn't seem like you. So, did she say what she's going to do?"

"You mean what she's going to say? She has to talk to them sooner or later. And yeah, she's going to tell them the truth."

"I was afraid of that. I don't suppose..."

"Don't even ask it. I told her to say whatever she wanted. It was a really shitty thing that you did, Dad."

His father sighed and there was a long silence before he spoke again. "I can understand that you both might see it that way. But I thought it was for the best at the time." He was quiet for another moment before adding, "Maybe I was mistaken."

"You're lucky that she's not going to press charges."

"She said that? Because of Helen I suppose. I guess I should be grateful for that at least."

"I would be."

"If she talks about this, you know my political career will be over."

"She won't be the one to blame," Cole said. He had zero sympathy for his father.

"Right. You're right. Well, I should go. Claire wants to watch some movie that starts in a few minutes. Call me when you're back in Charleston."

"Goodnight, Dad."

CHAPTER 35

L aura didn't stop the next day. She spoke to five different reporters by phone, telling them pretty much all the same thing. She didn't go into great detail but she did confirm that Cole's father had pretty much kidnapped her by sending her out to Montana. The reporters all seem surprised that she didn't want to press charges but she simply said that she wanted to put the past behind her. She also didn't want to go into any more detail about Aunt Helen than she needed to. Although she wasn't happy about the role Aunt Helen had played, Laura had grown close to her and they'd even started talking again recently. As strange as the situation was, she really did like the older woman.

Cole was due in about a half hour and Laura figured that she would just about have everything ready by then. She opened the oven and took a peek at the chicken Parmesan that was baking. The cheese was just beginning to melt. And the lemon cake was on the counter cooling.

She reached into a cabinet for a small bowl and dumped in a carton of vanilla frosting into it. Then she added a generous squeeze of lemon and a big handful of fresh raspberries and mixed it all together. She took a quick taste, added a little more lemon and it was perfect. After she frosted the cake, she tossed a salad together and set out plates and silverware on her small dining room table. It was a nice night, not too cool, so she thought maybe they'd sit outside and have a cocktail first like she and Tina used to do.

At six o'clock on the dot, there was a knock on the door. Laura walked towards feeling surprised by the rush of butterflies in her stomach. She tried to tell herself that it was ridiculous. It was just Cole. But she knew that things were different now. Everything had changed with both of their relationships, and now she had her memories back. Although Cole didn't know that yet.

"Come on in!" Laura opened the door wide. Cole walked in and gave her a hug.

"Something smells good!"

"Chicken Parmesan is in the oven. I hope that's okay?"

He looked at her little funny. "That's always been one of my favorites."

"Oh good! I thought we might sit outside for us to have a drink."

"Sure. Oh, I brought this for you. The girl at the store

said this one is popular." He handed her a bottle of wine, one of her favorite Chardonnays.

"Thank you. It's perfect!"

Laura poured drinks for both of them. A glass of wine for her and a bottle of beer for him. They took the drinks outside and sat on the two plastic chairs on her small balcony deck.

"So how did it go today? Did you like any of the places that you saw?" she asked.

"I did. The first two places were pretty sketchy and I was getting discouraged, but the last place she showed me was perfect. I gave her a check on the spot and as long as the background check comes through tomorrow, I'll be able to move in on Monday."

"Oh, that's perfect!"

"How did your day go? Did you talk to any of the reporters?"

"I did. I talked to about five of them. I was exhausted by the time I finished. But I think I gave them enough to keep them happy for a while."

"Hopefully it will die down soon and will be another story that interests them."

"They all asked about your father and if I plan to press charges. I told them no, which seemed to confuse them."

"Did they ask about Aunt Helen?"

"Just briefly. I really didn't go into much detail about anything. Oh, I did stress that you and I are just friends and there has been no cheating of any kind going on. I may have acted a bit outraged."

Cole laughed. "Thank you. I do appreciate that."

"So, are you hungry? We can head in and eat."

They went inside, and Laura dished out the chicken Parmesan onto two plates while Cole brought the bowl of salad to the table. He raved about her cooking as they ate. As they were just about finished Laura asked if he saved room for dessert.

"I always have room for dessert. What are we having?"

"An old favorite that I haven't had in a while. Lemon cake with lemon raspberry frosting."

Laura almost laughed at the look of shock on Cole's face.

"You remembered?" he asked softly. It was the first meal she'd ever cooked for him. She'd wanted to make his eighteenth birthday special and she knew chicken Parmesan and lemon cake were his favorites.

Laura smiled. "I remember pretty much everything now."

He still looked stunned. "When? Why didn't you tell me sooner?"

"It started when we went by the high school. But when you took me to the trailer park, the memories came rushing in and it was overwhelming. I didn't say anything then because I needed to process it all and because it just didn't feel right somehow. You were showing me around being so nice, and I thought you were happily married."

Laura paused for a moment. "And I was suddenly remembering how much I loved you and how in love we were. So, I didn't know what to say. I wanted to tell you but it just didn't feel like the right moment, if that makes sense?"

"It does. I can't begin to tell you how happy I am that you remember."

"I know. What we had was so special and so rare."

"I think that's partly why I married Chelsea. I dated a lot of girls after we broke up but none of them not even Chelsea made me feel the way that you did. I didn't think that I never find that kind of love again and I figured Chelsea was as close as I'd get."

"I probably never should've dated Dylan as long as I did. It was just easy and for a long time we did have fun together. But it was more serious for him than for me. You set a high bar."

Laura stood as a rush of emotion came over her and she felt her eyes water. She brought their plates to the sink and rinsed them as she fought back tears. She was just about to reach for the cake plates when she felt Cole's arms wrapped around her from behind. He turned her to face him and she caught her breath when she saw the look in his eyes.

"Laura, this might sound crazy but is there any chance..."

She nodded, and joy filled her heart as Cole brought his lips down to hers. It felt wonderful—natural and familiar at the same time. They kissed tentatively at first, tasting each other and finding their way back. And then they deepened the kiss and moved closer together. Laura breathed in his scent and sighed. Finally, she felt as though all was right in her world.

When they finally pulled apart, both of them were

speechless. Laura spoke first. "Are you ready for some cake?"

Cole laughed. "Sure, I'd love a piece."

They took the cake outside and ate on the balcony and talked for over an hour remembering old times. Until finally, it was dark and the air grew cold and they went back inside.

"I should probably head home soon I suppose," Cole said.

"Back to that sad motel room?" Laura smiled. "I have a better idea." She took his hand and pulled him toward her and a slow happy smile spread across his face.

"Are you sure? There is nothing in this world that I would want more than to stay here with you."

"We have a lot more catching up to do." Laura leaned in and kissed Cole lightly on the lips and then pulled him down the hall to her bedroom and shut the door behind them.

AFTER THE BEST night he'd had in years, Cole had an even better day after as he and Laura relaxed in her apartment all day, eating when they felt hungry, working on different songs together and more than once falling back into Laura's welcoming bed. For Cole, it was as if the lost years had disappeared and they were back to where they were, Laura and Cole. Laura seemed to feel it too.

Later that afternoon, when Cole was beginning to wonder if he'd worn out his welcome, Laura seemed to sense it. She came to him, wrapped her arms around him and after a long, sweet kiss said, "Why don't you check out of that hotel room, and stay here until Monday?" She didn't have to ask him twice.

He went back to the hotel and just as he was almost done packing everything up, Chelsea called.

"I talked to an attorney this morning. If we do a no-fault divorce there's a year waiting period. If we do fault, it's just ninety days. What do you think we should do? I had no idea about the one-year waiting period, did you?"

"I didn't think of it, but I should have remembered that. We can do fault. Tell them I cheated."

"Are you sure?" Chelsea sounded relieved.

"Yeah. It's in the papers, so we might as well go with it."

"Thank you. I really didn't want to wait a year."

"I know." Cole knew that once Chelsea had her mind made up, she was ready to move on and anxious to start dating Austin. And though he didn't like to think of it as cheating, since both he and Chelsea wanted the divorce, now that he and Laura had been together, it did qualify as adultery in the eyes of the court. South Carolina had a one-year separation policy for a no fault divorce and during that time dating was considered grounds for adultery, so it made sense to go with it. Neither one of them wanted to wait a whole year. Cole was ready to put his marriage behind him and move on to his future with Laura as soon as possible.

CHAPTER 36

The next few weeks were a whirlwind for Laura. She couldn't remember the last time she'd felt so happy. She saw Cole every day, and they spent just about every night together. He'd moved into his short-term rental, but still spent most evenings at her place, and occasionally she stayed at his. Dylan was still in the band. He'd been oddly supportive during the whole media frenzy and swore that it wasn't him that leaked the story. He'd said he knew that there was nothing to the rumors that she was dating Cole.

Laura didn't know what to think as she couldn't imagine who else would have. But, she didn't have any proof that it was him and for the time being, he wasn't being difficult to work with so it was easier to keep things going the way they were. She really didn't want to have to find a new band. All the other guys were great to work with.

They had a rare weekend off with no gigs anywhere and Laura was looking forward to spending it with Cole. They were planning to get some takeout and watch movies. He arrived a little after six carrying two huge paper bags of Chinese food. They spread everything on the coffee table and helped themselves. As they ate, Cole filled Laura in on how his day at the studio had gone.

"We recorded my new song today, and it went really well. Harry stopped by to check on us and he gave it two thumbs up. Said we may even want to go with it as my first single."

"Oh, that's so great!" Laura was thrilled for him and proud too. It was a really good song.

"I heard from Chelsea's lawyer today. Everything has been filed with the courts. So, if all goes well, we'll be divorced in about ninety days."

"Yeah, I heard about that earlier today too. I guess you haven't been online much today?"

Cole looked confused. "What are you talking about?"

"It's all over the news. With your father stepping down as governor last week, they must have had people still looking for anything to keep it going. They reported that Chelsea filed for divorce on grounds of adultery —with me."

"Oh no. I'm so sorry, Laura. I never wanted to drag you into this."

She put her hand on his. "I don't mind. I'm in this now and truthfully, I'd rather be out in the open about it. I don't want to sneak around anymore. I love you."

"I love you too. So much."

A loud knock at the door startled both of them.

"Are you expecting anyone?" Cole asked.

"No, I have no idea who it is." Laura got up and walked to the door and opened it a crack to see who was there. Dylan shoved the door open and stepped inside, looking manically around the room until he saw Cole.

"So, it is true!" he yelled, and that's when Laura saw the gun, tucked into his jeans. She flashed a panicked warning look at Cole to stay calm.

"What are you doing here, Dylan?" she asked quietly.

"I saw the news today, and I had to come here to see for myself. So, you were cheating on me after all, with him. I knew it!"

"Dylan, calm down. I never cheated on you. Ever. Cole and I only got back together recently, well after we broke up."

Suddenly, the gun was in Dylan's hands. "I don't believe you. I saw the news. The divorce papers say adultery and that Cole cheated."

Cole spoke up as he slowly stood from the table and took a step toward them. "That's just a technicality. So we could get a faster divorce. We'd have to wait a year otherwise."

"But you were going to cheat!"

"I had no intention of cheating. My wife and I both wanted the divorce. She wants to move on as much as I do."

"You ruined everything! Laura was supposed to marry me!"

"Put the gun down, Dylan. You don't want to do this,"

Cole tried to reason with him. But it only seemed to make things worse.

"Don't tell me what I want! I know what I want. I want you out of the way so I can have Laura back."

"I don't think that's going to happen," Cole said.

"Oh yeah?" Dylan lifted his gun and aimed at Cole. He wasn't paying any attention to Laura, and she acted without thinking, jumping on his back to try to knock him down. It worked, except his gun went off and Laura's heart sank when she heard a blood-curdling scream from Cole. But a moment later, Cole was right there beside her and grabbed the gun from Dylan while Laura sat on his back to keep him down.

Cole pointed the gun at his face while Laura called 911. When the gun went off, it grazed the side of Cole's thigh. Enough to hurt, but hopefully it wasn't too serious. The cops and an ambulance arrived a few minutes later, and the medics attended to Cole while the police talked to Laura and put Dylan into handcuffs. One of the two officers, a woman in her forties named Deb, recognized him.

"Up to your old tricks again, I see. I hoped that we wouldn't run into you again. I believe you are still on probation. You know what that means?"

"What does that mean?" Laura asked. "What is he on probation for?"

"This charmer has a history of domestic violence. He's at the end of a five-year probationary period but this latest incident is going to automatically toss him right back into jail and the sentence will be much stricter this time."

"Oh! I had no idea."

"Yeah, you literally dodged a bullet this time. But you should be safe now. We'll take care of him from here."

Laura watched as took Dylan away. She then followed the ambulance to the hospital and waited with Cole while he was seen. It was just a graze, so he just needed a few stitches and a few hours later, they were on their way home. Once they were back at Laura's place, she made them both a cup of tea and put away all the food that was still sitting out. They snuggled together on the sofa, with Cole's sore leg propped up on the coffee table.

"What a night. How are you doing? Are you okay?" he asked.

"I'm fine. It was shocking to see Dylan like that, but it's also a relief that he's out of our life now. I had no idea about his history."

"How would you know?" Cole asked.

"It's scary. He was so friendly, charming even, at first. It really wasn't until we'd been together for a long time that I started to see that side of him. It's why I ended things with him. I knew it would only get worse."

"Well, he's gone now. We can sleep like babies tonight."

Laura laughed. "I always sleep well as long as I'm with you."

"Me too."

THE NEXT MORNING while Laura was still sleeping. Cole called his father. "Dad, there's something I need you to do for me, immediately."

CHAPTER 37

Two days later, the FedEx package arrived from Cole's father. He opened it and then called Laura.

"I think it's time we went out in public together. Let's go to dinner and then to hear some live music. What do you think?"

"I'd love to!"

Cole asked around for suggestions on where to go and made a reservation for them at Etch restaurant. When they arrived, he knew that it was a great choice. The atmosphere was romantic and energetic. It was a very busy place with servers bustling around a packed dining room. They were led to a quiet corner table and Cole couldn't take his eyes of Laura.

She looked more beautiful than ever in an elegant black dress that hugged her slim curves. She wore her hair pulled back halfway with the rest tumbling down her back.

He had to resist the urge to run his hands through it. He'd dressed for the occasion too, wearing one of his favorite button-down shirts and an aqua silk tie.

They put their dinner orders in and a short while later, while sipping their drinks and sharing a roasted cauliflower appetizer, Cole decided that it was time. He stood up, walked over to Laura and got down on one knee.

At first, Laura was confused. "Cole what are you doing? Are you alright? Is it your leg?"

Cole laughed. "No, my leg is fine now." He reached for one of Laura's hands. "Laura, I love you more than ever, more than I thought it was possible to love someone. I never stopped loving you and I never will. I don't want to waste another moment. Will you marry me? As soon as the divorce is final of course." He grinned and then held his breath, waiting for her answer. He didn't have to wait long. Her eyes welled up immediately, and she simply said, "Of course I'll marry you. You're the love of my life, Cole Dawson."

Cole felt his own eyes tear up a little as he reached into his pocket, pulled out the ring and slid it onto Laura's finger. When she saw it, the tears fell. "How did you? I don't understand...."

Cole stood, took both of her hands and pulled her in for a quick kiss before explaining.

"I called my father a few days ago. I realized that he must have the ring. That he had to have taken it when you were in the hospital so that you wouldn't ask any questions or remember me."

Laura held her hand up and marveled at the sparkling small diamond. "It's perfect. Now it's where it should be."

"For always and forever," Cole agreed.

EPILOGUE

FOUR YEARS LATER....

Riley and Reba Dawson, you're not leaving this table until you each have three more bites of those peas."

"How about one bite? Just one?" Reba, ever the negotiator, asked with an adorable smile. Her twin sister Riley nodded in agreement.

Laura sighed. "All right, two bites. But that's my final offer." She watched as her three-year-old daughters both held their noses as they each ate one pea at a time, until they'd had two. They were too much.

"Okay, off with the both of you. Go play." She cleared the dishes while Cole poured them each a glass of wine. It was a rare Friday night that she wasn't performing somewhere. She and Cole went into the family room with their wine so they could relax and keep an eye on the girls who were very busy building something with a pile of pink

Legos. She glanced out the window where the sun was just starting to set and a rosy glow covered the sky. She loved where they lived now.

Soon after they'd married which was immediately after the divorce was final, they moved into this house in a great Nashville neighborhood. It was new when they bought it and had a nice yard and lots of windows to let in the light. It wasn't big, but it had three bedrooms which was plenty of room for their growing family. It was Laura's favorite place to be. Home with her husband and children.

Once they married, Laura's career had taken off like a rocket. Instead of hurting them, the media coverage of what happened to Laura and Cole only made them even more loved, especially when they got married. She was invited to be a permanent judge on the talent show she and Cole had been on and that made her a household name and her earnings soared even higher.

Her only worry was that it never happened for Cole. His album fizzled. The public never really embraced it. He made a second one and performed with Laura many times, but even though the second album did a little better, it wasn't enough for Black Duck to want to continue working with him.

Cole said he didn't mind, and he seemed to mean it. As his music career was winding down, he decided to study for the bar in Tennessee and once he passed it, he started overseeing Laura's contracts and eventually took on other local artists and carved out a specialty in entertainment law.

He seemed to enjoy it and although he had a small

office downtown, he mostly worked from home, or on the road if Laura was touring. The girls were small enough that they could all tour as a family. She knew that would change once the girls started school and by then she knew she'd want to cut back on the touring too. But for now, it was working well for them.

And Aunt Helen was still in their lives. She came to visit every year around the holidays and stayed with them for a few days. She adored her 'grandchildren' and was the closest thing to a grandmother that the girls had.

"Penny for your thoughts," Cole said as he put his arm around her and pulled her close. She snuggled against him and sighed.

"All happy thoughts. I was just thinking how lucky we are to have found our way back to each other and to have the life that we have with our girls."

"WE ARE LUCKY," Cole agreed. He kissed Laura lightly on the forehead and smiled as he watched Riley and Reba playing together. The girls were fraternal twins and were very different in appearance and personality. Riley looked more like Laura and was sweet and quiet while Reba looked more like him and was the feisty one. He loved them both equally and fiercely and was very protective of all three of his girls.

And he agreed with Laura. It had taken them a while to find their way back to each other, but now that they had, their life was about as good as he ever could have imagined it would be. Laura was so talented and humble. He knew that she felt guilty sometimes that his career had never taken off the way that hers did.

He was disappointed at first, but he also came to realize that it was different for him. He enjoyed music, but he didn't have the same all-consuming passion for it or the true innate talent that Laura did. He actually enjoyed the law, and he was grateful to his father for pushing him to go on to law school. Because it had turned out to be a good back up plan. Once he started handling Laura's affairs word spread and clients started coming to him, some of them pretty famous too with complicated contracts and financial affairs that needed attending to.

Every year, things got a little better with his father, too. He was mellowing out as he grew older. Resigning from public office was probably one of the best things that could have happened to him, even though he didn't see it that way at the time. He stopped craving power and started appreciating what he had more and Cole knew a lot of that was due to Claire who he married soon after he resigned. She had always been one very good influence on him and the other was the girls. They'd changed his father considerably.

He was now a doting grandfather who spoiled them rotten whenever he saw them, which wasn't nearly as often as he'd like. But Charleston was a hike from Nashville. They usually saw each other on the holidays. Cole and Laura would drive to Charleston with the girls and every few months, his father and Claire would drive to Nashville to spend a few days. They always stayed at the Hermitage

Hotel, one of Nashville's most luxurious, as there wasn't a spare room for them and Cole knew it was easier for all of them if they had their own space.

His father was friendly towards Laura now and had even apologized which Laura graciously accepted. Cole knew that she wasn't thrilled with the idea of spending any time with him initially, but when she saw how he was with the girls and how much they loved him, she accepted it.

"Have I told you I love you yet today? I don't think I have," he asked Laura as he reached for his wine.

She laughed. "No not yet. You're slacking apparently."

He grinned. "Well, I love you, today and always."

"And I love you, today and always."

The familiar saying always made him smile. They said it to each other every day without fail.

He leaned over and kissed her and then they relaxed together, watching the girls play and the sun slowly set. Life was good.

NOTE TO READERS...

I hope you enjoyed Laura and Cole's story. This book was a labor of love for me. I first started working on this story over two years ago. During that time, I've written other books, among them Cute Cowboy, which is Lily and Cody's story.

You may have noticed a mention of Lily in the book. Laura first makes an appearance in Cute Cowboy when

Lily comes to Nashville for a visit. It's part of the Rivers End Ranch series.

My most recent book in that series is Billionaire's Baby. It's a fun story about billionaire Ben who is now caring for his niece Taylor and is desperately in need of a nanny. Anna needs money for law school tuition since her evil step-mother kicked her out of the house and her father's will.

Up next.....my next book in the River's End Ranch series will be out on March 26, Teasing Tammy. Charming doctor Clark falls hard for bookstore manager Tammy. He doesn't get off to a good start when he sets off to the bookstore determined to ask her out and instead ends up bringing her to the ER with a broken foot....and it's kind of his fault.

Thanks so much for reading! If you'd like an email when I have a new release, please sign up here for my list!

And click here to see all my books on Amazon.

Thank you so much, and Happy Reading!

~Pam

Printed in Great
Britain
by Amazon